THE COMPLEAT PURGE

$14.95
978-0-9846475-5-2
0-9846475-5-4
THE COMPLEAT PURGE
BY TRISHA LOW

(C) KENNING EDITIONS FOR TRISHA LOW
OCTOBER, 2013

COVER DESIGN BY JEFF CLARK / QUEMADURA
INTERIOR COMPOSITION BY PATRICK DURGIN

DISTRIBUTED TO INDIVIDUALS AND THE TRADE BY
SMALL PRESS DISTRIBUTION
1341 SEVENTH STREET
BERKELEY, CA 94710-1409
1-800-869-7553
SPDBOOKS.ORG

KENNINGEDITIONS.COM

THE COMPLEAT
PURGE

Trisha Low

VOL. I: THE LAST WILL & TESTAMENT OF TRISHA LOW

for Joey Yearous—Algozin, who raised me.

'The man is dead but not dead enough. When she hits him with a stick we see she is in fact attached to him. So here's the issue. When a fatherless woman leaves home she'll have to deal with the fact that she's stuck on a dead man. It's a risky situation—the two elder daughters end up dead.'

—Lewis Hyde

'i believe in not ever telling anybody anything, but somehow i don't think that excludes also telling everybody everything.'

—rgr-pop.tumblr.com

In Memory of Trisha Low
(1988-1994)

Last Will & Testament of Trisha Low

I, Trisha Low of Singapore, Singapore, The World, The Milky Way, The Universe declare that this is my Last Will & Testament.

Article I
Preliminary Declarations

Dear Mommy and Daddy and Marsha,

    If you are reading this then it means that I am dead. I am very sorry. It's OK though because I still love you a lot. It is Wednesday today and I had a good day but I saw the flood on TV where two tents and a sleeping bag got washed away so just in case! I also saw one of the tents catch fire even though Mrs. Chan at school told us wet things are not supposed to burn. Here are some things I want because even though I know little girls do not tell adults what to do because I guess if I am dead then it is like I'm already an adult.

Article II
Specific Bequests and Devises

1. Marsha should have the $1 I got from the tooth fairy yesterday even though the tooth fairy also gave her $1 for just being my little sister
2. She can also have my pink power ranger because it is better than her yellow one.
3. Mommy can have my jewelry but not the scrunchie with the green crayons in it.
4. Daddy can have everything else.
5. Caroline can also have my books and my Minnie Mouse night-light because she is scared of the dark and still drinks milk out of a baby bottle. Also maybe my hair clips because she is going to look weird until all her hair grows back.

I have to go now. Mommy you are telling me I have to go to Chinese tuition before I'm late. Hope you find this if you need to!

Love,
Trisha

General Provisions

If any beneficiary or beneficiaries of this Will shall contest my Will or in any manner attempt to have it, or any trust or beneficial interest created by it declared invalid, such person or persons shall receive no benefits from or interests under this Will and my Will shall be carried out as if such person or persons had pre-deceased me.

I have entered neither into a contract to make wills nor into a contract not to revoke wills. Any similarity of the provisions of my Will to the provisions of the will of any other person, if any, executed on the same or on different dates than my Will, shall not be construed of as evidence of such a contract.

Unless specifically set forth in writing and acknowledged by the donee thereof, any gift I have made or will make during my lifetime shall not be treated as satisfaction, in whole or in part, of any device or bequest in my Will.

On this 8th day of February 1994, in the City of New York, State of New York, I hereby sign this document and declare it to be my last will.

In Memory of Trisha Low
(1988-2001)

Last Will & Testament of Trisha Low

I, Trisha Low of High Wycombe, Buckinghamshire, England, Great Britain declare that this is my Last Will & Testament.

Article I
Preliminary Declarations

Dear Mom, Dad and Marsha,

I think it's quite a nice feeling to know that in a couple of hours I'll be gone.

I mean, yeah, I know I have to make you go through all my stuff which is kind of a complete waste of time, and I know it'll make you sad but it's still...nice. I'm really sorry. I do love you guys, you know. I guess I just wanted to let you know. I'll say what I'm supposed to say, too—I'm sorry to create a grievous situation for you and regret deeply that my decision will cause you great sadness.

Right now my Christmas cake from cookery weighs a ton and I don't know how I'm going to get it home without killing it so I figured maybe I would just give up.

... Lottie says the mouse figurine on it looks like it's dead.

I don't think that's a good thing.

I don't know.

It's like there's this massive something on your head/heart/soul and it's telling you things you don't want to know, some sort of silent whisper in your head.

... It's like I wish I were going mad.
School is killing me.

And i suppose it would be okay if you just abandoned me and left me to die. I guess it kind of feels like you already did.
... I wish it would snow again.

Chapel was cancelled because of the weather and we went out to play on the lacrosse pitches. We didn't have a sled so we used the 'warning, no walking on the grass' signs instead.

They make remarkably good sleds.

Anyway. It was fun. And then it was over.

But they're putting salt on our snow and ruining it.

You know what?

I don't care any more. I just don't care any more.

If I don't give a damn, then there's really nothing left to do, is there?

I'm grateful. You've both given me everything I could have asked for.

But at this point it's just too strange coming back to people you only used to know.

Someone once said 'I'd never jump from a building; too much time to regret.' But regret what? Killing yourself? Your life? Fucking up? There's too much in this world we assume.

Death always has that tempting, glossed over glamour to it, some romanticism in slitting your wrists, or even stepping off the edge of the eiffel tower, but this feels difficult. Still clean though. Easy.

If you find this it probably means you'll know eventually too about the exacto knife I keep under my pillow so I guess I feel I should explain. I want to say I'm sorry but I'm not. Everything seems so insignificant, like you're estranged from everything, floating on air and somehow, it seems to make you view the world...differently. I guess I was trying to cut all the bad out of me.

Sometimes, it seems, you dare yourself to dabble in fate, and death, and you wonder what it would be like; that first slash to the wrist, or the wavering between decision and doubt before so you do it anyway. The first time I did it I turned and stabbed my own arm. It didn't break the skin and I kept going and going until it went through the skin and I pulled it out and all the blood started trickling down my arm and I just watched it and it felt like it was releasing the pressure in my head, like releasing all the bad blood and maggots. I knew it wasn't (maggots and stuff) but it was to me. When I've been in that state I've come out of there disgusted and when I got back to the house I've cut again. When there is no feeling when you're dead inside, the pain, the blood, it proves I am alive. Red and beautiful and I can feel again. It's like I said to Aggie, I said it's sad you know, the way nothing strikes me any more, and she said, baby, you just gotta find something you really want to feel.

You know what? I really have to stop this. Really Really Really have to stop this. Stop trying to convince myself that its not going to hurt anyone if no one knows, or that it's all right if it's helping me cope or with my grades or anything. Because it doesn't. And it's stupid and if anyone ever found out again, I'd know that I was being horribly selfish and stupid and I hate that. So I must stop. But it's satisfaction. Like when you find the right vein and there's blood enough to get down your wrist, but not enough to kill you. People live their life on edge in other ways, this is how I live mine.

Article II
Specific Bequests and Devises

When I'm gone, all my books are to be shared out among gaiatri, kim-mei, caroline, wei, andrea and janice. And those they don't want can go to my sister but it's not like she'll want them really cause she hates me

My scrapbook you can keep and my comics can go to andrea even though she's not really obsessed with x-man any more. I suppose tash and lottie could decide between themselves who gets what out of the rest of my manga.

My cds can go to caroline and the books for catechism and my bible to gaiatri and she gets my marvin plushie too, just to annoy her.

Caroline can have my dad's giant shirts and my huge scary jumpers. And wei can have my sketchbooks. (hey, they can be re-used, ok?) and kim-mei my notebooks, i suppose.

Yeah. I guess now I won't have to revise for Chemistry. Mom, this has nothing to do with my relationship with Christ. I believe in God's Word, and I love Christ and the sacrifice he made for me. I intend to serve Him until my last minute, but I can't serve him in this world any longer. I know you won't understand that, so it will have to be between me and God.

That's all I can say.

… Sorry but I'm not sorry for not being sorry? What I am I'm sorry for is the grief this will cause you and hope that you will always love me the same…

Trisha

P.S. In case you need to get into anything.
Email password: dollcollector.
The key to my lockbox: underwear drawer—school dresser, top right.
UK bank account pin-code: 2189.
Locker combination: 65-47-22.

Article III
Executor and Administrative Powers

Dear Lottie,

This is going to be depressing.

I have that terrible sick feeling in my stomach that means I'm probably leaving. And if you're reading this, then I'm gone. I wanted to say, I'm really sorry. I know you tried your best to take care of me.

This conversation went on in the common room before I went out yesterday:

Me: I'm going out to High Wycombe this weekend, do you want me to get you guys anything?

Harriet: Um…

Cami: A life.

Georgie: A boyfriend.

Me: …right, i'll get you guys doughnuts.

… I do not know one boy who's over the age of ten. Not one.

I'm hurting so much at the moment, what with leaving and being lonely and unloved here in school. On the one hand, I don't know how you put up with me, moody little cow that I am, and I know you'd call me self-deprecating, but I still insist I'm not. And really, I love the way you give me advice even if you know I won't listen just because it makes me feel better.

And I love the way we talk about things no one else understands, and argue about morbidity and diaries, and how we put ridiculous amounts of sugar in our tea… So why do i pretend to be some-one i'm not? I have to stop pretending I'm someone I'm not, stop doing things to make people happy even though I'm slowly fading inside, into someone I don't even know at all.

What's happened to the real trisha?

It scares me that I don't even know any more. Call me stupid/sentimental, but it's just funny how.

...the four right chords can no longer make me cry.

I don't want people to be upset because of me, but it's even worse when you can't do anything about it. This is just something I have to do.

So, i'm happy, now, I think, I hope.
I have to be the most screwed up person there is. Ever.

As for the rest of them. Tell them to go ahead and judge me, they can take their best shot now it doesn't matter. Here's to you, my dear, and here's some comfort:

the halls of my mind are so narrow
each time I pass you, my love
our shoulders kiss and I wonder
if you have not died and left
your skeleton behind.

perhaps this is the only way
we are allowed to bleed,
with lips smiling as if split in two
the edges of your heart
ragged;
nobody smiles in this house
the clock has hid its face
in its hands
and the pendulums are heavyhearted

but love, i will be forever a dreamer
and so will you,
if you will let me take you by the hand
(and by the heartstrings)
sobriquets murmured sleepily
and let me tell you how
not everything is gone
we still have

our hearts in our chests
and breath in our bodies (not much, enough)
and hands to hold (even cold ones will do)
and magic
that pulses through us and fades.

Article IV
Guardianship Provisions

Dear Edd,

I can't offer much of an explanation, but here are some shards and a thing I wrote this last night. If you're reading this, I guess I'm gone. And I'm sorry, I really am. But you're the one thing, I think, the only thing I'm sad to leave.

I tried so hard to make you smile. says:
I suppose he doesn't like me enough
Perhaps self-destruction is the answer. says:
Why did he kiss you? I mean, isn't he like, with Aggie? Aren't they all like, in love and shit?
I tried so hard to make you smile. says:
She's having a hard time and he's taking it really rough.
Perhaps self-destruction is the answer. says:
But! Does that mean he likes you?
I tried so hard to make you smile. says:
I don't know, we were apart from the group, a little, and we were talking.
Perhaps self-destruction is the answer. says:
Fuck, do you mean he likes you?
Perhaps self-destruction is the answer. says:
And something happened?
Perhaps self-destruction is the answer. says:
What what what?

The night is wet when she steps into its arms, soaked and sodden from a frozen, pent-up season; she watches rain dance on the black tarmac, looks for her reflection but sees only ghosts. Hands in her pockets, hair streaming water from her collar of her shirt and her skin, she looks up to the sky. Starless nights. Long stretches on broken couches with a guitar. Brown envelopes on desks, old love songs on the radio, rhythm on roof.

People kiss in books and memories that never happened, on cinema screens, on the corners of streets. She leans her head on the door, while the streetlamps flicker, and turns down her walkman, listening to the secrets of the storm. Nothing yields. There is just a sky too open to love, a street. a road too silent to follow. The sky blurs into a mass of light.

She leaves lonely handprints on windows, tries to be useful, makes conversation, draws unseen stars in the corners of her papers. In six thousand years, tonight will be invisible. Maybe she already is.

She falls in love with his hands first, the slim delineation of his bones, the delicacy with which he positions his drum. This is beauty, pouring from him, saturating the room; this is beauty, in the way he moves and breathes, the wonder of him. He is proud on his stool, straight-spined as he begins to drum, hat slouched over his eyes. He plays as if he'll never play again.

There's a realness about him that she's almost forgotten to memorise, the youthfulness in his laugh and his smile, the imperfection of the sun rising, unfettered and free.

Everyone she knows; cut out of sepia tinged photos, and she the same, walking sideways, with hurt imprinted in her eyes and she knows

she's never met anyone so real.

It's probably asking too much, but take care of Aggie. I know it killed you when she almost left last month. I'm sorry, really, I am. I love you, more that you know, more than you'll ever care to.

Love,
Trisha.

General Provisions

If any beneficiary or beneficiaries of this Will shall contest my Will or in any manner attempt to have it, or any trust or beneficial interest created by it declared invalid, such person or persons shall receive no benefits from or interests under this Will and my Will shall be carried out as if such person or persons had pre-deceased me.

I have entered neither into a contract to make wills nor into a contract not to revoke wills. Any similarity of the provisions of my Will to the provisions of the will of any other person, if any, executed on the same or on different dates than my Will, shall not be construed of as evidence of such a contract.

Unless specifically set forth in writing and acknowledged by the donee thereof, any gift I have made or will make during my lifetime shall not be treated as satisfaction, in whole or in part, of any device or bequest in my Will.

On this 9th day of November, 2001, in the City of New York, State of New York, I hereby sign this document and declare it to be my last will.

In Memory of Trisha Low
(1988-2003)

Last Will & Testament of Trisha Low

I, Trisha Low of High Wycombe, Buckinghamshire, England, Great Britain declare that this is my Last Will & Testament.

Article I
Preliminary Declarations

Dear Mommy and Daddy (and Marsha),

Thinking of who I've been, who I'm supposed to be, and who the fuck I am now. 1 year, 20 years, 50 years, I'm so many people within a single day, from thought to thought, i don't know what to think of this current manifestation. I'm not happy. It's been so dark for so long and right now I don't see how anything will even become illuminated Something inside of me went away. The air is sweet and everything seems so intricately simple, like woven nets and sand and the sky burning blue above me, burning straight onto my heart like a branding of new life and new beginnings and I don't want it. I don't believe it. Every day there are people telling me I can do anything. I can be anyone. My friends are acting like they're ready for embellishments and sun-kissed skin and laughter and they smile and tell me there are empty pages filling with my words and I don't even care. People keep saying to me that I'm ready to look and I'm ready to see, ready to live, ready to be. But in the grander scheme of things, who even gives a fuck.

Because really, I'm sick of eating. I feel so fat all the time. Like I did so good in the morning! I had 2 glasses of calorie burning tea, and six grapes. Then Lottie asked me to go see a movie with her, and of course my self-control failed and I ate popcorn. It was a small and it didn't have any butter on it, but still. Then I had some of her candy during the movie and I couldn't stop saying to myself 'oh my god you idiot.' Then later that night I had dinner at the Bevans and had salad that probably had caloric dressing, a huge roll, and a chicken leg. And then, I got back to school, it was Tasha's birthday so ate half a cake delight brownie cake. The whole thing had 370 calories. I feel so guilty. And to make things worse, I have no motivation to get to the basement and jump it off with my skipping rope. All I am having today is two protein shakes and as much tea as I can choke down. I want to be skinny, but I'm so tired of thinking about eating and when I'm not eating all I can think about is what I'm allowed to. All I want is to put my hand on my waist and feel it resting in the hollow between my hip and my ribs.

I literally feel like I don't know how to be human. Like, do you ever get that feeling where you don't want to talk to anybody? You don't want to smile and you don't want to fake being happy. But at the same time you don't know exactly what's wrong either. There isn't a way to explain it to someone who doesn't already understand. If you could want anything in the world it would be to be alone. People have stopped being comforting and being along never was. At least when you're alone no one will constantly ask you what's wrong and there isn't anyone who won't take 'I don't know' for an answer. You feel the way you do just because and it doesn't feel like it's going to pass any time soon.

I'm 100% miserable. I HATE. I HATE how I'm so WEAK and SELFISH and I HATE how there's no one I can tell. I blacked out after the school concert and it sucked because the band played so well and I couldn't even celebrate. I hate myself. I'm cold in the middle of summer. Everything feels like it's falling out in my fingertips. I keep writing all the way up my forearm because I think it'll at least make me stop cutting because I feel like the worst daughter in the world, and I know it really hurts you guys but I'm just not ready to get better. I still oil my blade every week. We did lino prints at school and I just kept driving my tools into my hand. I have at least 5 cuts that are like at least 4 millimeters deep and I'm not joking. I looked at a ruler. My eyes are dull. My heart spasms and makes my chest ache.

Waking up nauseous is one of the worst things next to waking up still breathing, which is crazy because I'm going to end up throwing up anyway. I just can't be bothered any more. I think I've been a pretty good daughter even if I've turned into a complete brat and I just don't want to make things worse for you guys any more. So if you read this, I'm sorry, I love you, but it just all got to be so pointless for me and I couldn't stand it any more I want everything and nothing I don't feel well at all.

Trisha.

Article II
Specific Bequests and Devises

I guess you guys will have to deal with all my stuff—but just make sure for me, please, that these people get these things:

Tasha:

~Breakfast on Pluto DVD
~The Chronicles of Narnia: The Lion, The Witch and The Wardrobe DVD
~(This is embarrassing, but) Harry Potter and The Goblet of Fire book (British edition)
~King Kong DVD
~The Corpse Bride DVD
~Lord of War DVD
~Revolver DVD
~The Lords of Dogtown (for that blonde boy in Elephant, she thinks he's really cute)

Slaine:

~A History of Violence DVD
~The Brothers Grimm DVD
~Domino DVD(I know, Keira Knightley, but bounty hunters)
~The Legend of Zorro DVD
~My William Blake collected poems

Lottie:

~My 2 Libertines albums
~2 Yeti EPs
~Dirty Pretty Things album
~Babyshambles album
~Libertines poster
~Yeti poster and shirt
~Dresden Dolls piano score
~Iggy Pop Raw Power album
~Everything by or involving The Cure
~Guitar stickers (all of them)
~3 Strokes albums
~2 The Damn Personals albums

~3 The Cure albums
~all the rest of my DVDs (see the separate lists for others)
~all the rest of my books—make sure she gets the TS Eliot, Auden, Baudelaire, Rimbaud and Byron
~Her and Tasha can split all of my comics and merch between them

Aggie:

~All my black and red Tshirts
~Black cord overalls
~Red and black striped tights
~PVC platforms
~Braids with red ribbons (thin)
~All my Lime Crime Makeup (Dolly I)
~All the false lashes from Cyberdog
~Long skirts (the uneven lacy and suit velvet)
~Boots
~Lacy knee socks
~fishnets
~Top hat
~bunny ears
~corset
~lolita skirt
~shirt + tie with the hospital print
~Petticoat
~lolita/cobain sunglasses

Marsha:

~all of my nicer clothing
~really, anything she wants.

Thank you. I love you guys a lot and I'm sorry. There are just too many little girls in symmetry and I'm sick and tired of being all out of a row.

Love,
Trisha.

P.S. In case you need to get into anything.
Email password: dollcollector.
The key to my lockbox: underwear drawer—school dresser, top right.
UK bank account pin-code: 2189.
Locker combination: 65-47-22.

Article III
Executor and Administrative Powers

Dear Lottie:

I hope: too much in some things.

I hear: music in your words.

I crave: brown eyes and cds I can't have and nutella.

I regret: all together too much.

I cry: for the four right chords.

I care: more than those I care about too.

I always: worry too much.

I believe: in rock 'n' roll.

I feel: alone and insecure.

I listen: when the words grab hold of me and won't let go.

I hide: in apathy.

I drive: you crazy.

I sing: quietly and hopelessly off-key

I dance: behind closed doors.

I write: but it's never quite enough.

I play: guitar. bass. make-believe.

I miss: being sure about everything.

I search: for things I lack

I learn: too much, too late.

I feel: your words pounding in my head.

I know: you're out there, somewhere out there.

I say: things I don't mean.

I succeed: (never.)

I dream: of things so impossible.

I wonder: at this fucking amazing world and wonder why I can't be a part of it.

I want: not much, just more of everything.

I have: awesome friends.

I give: myself to lost causes.

I fall: (falling. Will someone catch me?)

I fight: for the revolution, any revolution.

I need: something else to get me through this semi-charmed kind of life, baby, baby.

You never write a song with a happy ending. And know what? For once in my life, I really do think tomorrow will be sunny. Just not here.

It's just one of those days when I can't think, I can't write, I can't talk, and really, I feel absolutely rubbish. And I've been having a lot of these days lately, so I'm wondering what the hell's wrong with me and coming up with a big fat zilch. The people I've grown to trust, I don't any more, apart from you. The only people who really stay constant I worry about bothering, and that's so screwed up because I know they have problems of their own, and my own selfishness isn't really going to help anything, and it sucks. I hate being self centered and I hate being stupid like this, and I hate how the closer I get to some people, the further away I'll be from others, and this could be going to be just another unsent letter that no one's ever going to see. Or maybe not. Ha.

Fuck it. I'm giving in. This is the last time, I promise, I always promise I won't do it, but I haven't felt this fucking rotten in a long long time. It's like needing a fix, you start shaking, and thoughts run through your head, and you think, no no, let's scare the demons away, but they don't, and all you want is a bloody razor. I hate it when I feel like this, it's not like anything else but sheer desperation and selfishness, but it feels like it's going to explode in my face, so what maybe I should just let it.

If I do, just know. I love you.

Trisha

PS. Keep my diary away from my parents, will you. You know where it is.

Article IV
Guardianship Provisions

Dear Edd,

Whatever.

I suppose every circus must have its clown.

you're a thief like all the rest only your price is knowledge;
every circus must have it's urchin boys, and you're the one
picking at my pocket, beggar asking me for scraps
well here, take this, roll over, good girl, sit, stay. You may
hold the cards and hold your hand around my heart but squeeze
while you can, pet, because your gypsy bag of tricks is almost

all

played

out

oh yes, each book spins out another day & night but not everything
turns out like scherezade, my pet; my grin like a knife hangs above
your head and one day you'll be nothing but a half-smile to them, pet
one day you'll run out of stories to tell;

i was a child then; some say i still am
and will be forever. i was a dreamer then.
i know how to smile, yes; this doesn't mean
i don't have any regrets. things like—

(if i start i will never finish)

and then it ends all over again.

You confuse me so much it's not even funny. I don't know if it's some sort of ploy or you just can't
make up your mind, but it just seems you're screwing with both of us and it's not a good thing. I'm

perfectly content being your little sister figure, like what you told me a long time ago, I was happy for you and Aggie, and still am, told you both that if you ever hurt each other, I'd hunt you down and kill you. And I liked you, and it was nice, when we did crazy things like sit in tattoo shops to people-watch and you say I should get wings on my wrist, but then again it's far too symbolic. But then we walk down Camden street alone, and you take my hand and say, actually, I'm not so much of a little sister, really, and it's times like that I don't know what to do apart from kiss you again and feel guilty later.

It's one of those freeze-frame moments in time where everything's moving so slowly it feels it's sepia tinted; strange.

After all, we learnt to talk from movies, and it's nice to pretend we're living one, that everything's going to be okay, we all get our fairytale beginnings in the end. But the one perfect slide in a tangled reel doesn't go very far at all, it's all rain tapping on the rooftop, foggy fingerprints on the window, a cheek against cool glass. It's the simpler things in life, the most perfect song in the world playing on the stereo, the feel of people beside you you can trust, when things fall into place and you know that finally you don't have to pretend any more because the earth's infinite capacity to hope is overwhelming in the room, and it's because of you.

Somehow, all that just doesn't feel like my life at all but it is, when I'm with you and it is infinitely more than anything I could think of, and you couple that with foreign intoxication and at the end of it all there's balance and it's like being objective doesn't matter anymore, practicality is redundant and it seems like everything suddenly becomes real.

And all I can think about is how I would give anything in the world for things to stay how they were when we're alone, to keep sharing perfect moments with perfect people - this is the sort of confessional morning where all I want to do is say yes.

This morning all I want to be is in love. But it's so much, you're too much, and you're not here. And so, maybe this is the best day for me to be gone.

I love you, I do. I'll miss you.

Article V
Testamentary Trusts for Minor Child(ren)

Take care of Tor, won't you. She was a little girl and we made her into an adult, she grew up too fast and she's fourteen, older than a little old woman, with ideas in her head and it's all our fault. She's grown up now, so old at 13. She's grown up now, with tears in her eyes, and I don't know what to do when she says i wish this was a dream and why can't why can't I wake up now?

And she, with hands in her sleeves and hurt in her face doesn't want to, she loses her years like buttons or leaves, but they never come back and she's always the same, doesn't want to change. Her holding on to us, the way we are, the way we deal with everything, is costing her everything. I feel like it's cost me everything and for me it's getting easier and easier to disappear from this world and now it's easy and I'm just giving up and letting go.

She can't turn into us, not her, with the laughter she brings, the comfort of her presence, but she lives in her unease, never knows her worth, sings like a nightingale pretends to be a sparrow, draws visions of heaven and puts them down to hell, doesn't pray doesn't show doesn't tell, I never know with her and yet I always do, and this one no one can afford to lose. So again, I love you. Take care of her and don't let things turn out for her or for you, the way it did for Aggie, or for me.

Trisha

Dear Tor,

Hey. Um. Basically, I know I haven't really been there for you lately and I really shouldn't let my work get in the way, but I just wanted you to know, you know, I still love you. I'm sorry I'm gone, and I know it'll seem like I've just abandoned you, but really, I just…couldn't any more. But I care for you so fucking much. And if you ever have anything to talk about, you should go talk to Aggie or Edd or even Lottie. Because I know this school is an arse, and you'll only be here another year, and everyone's really going to miss you when you go, and things are going to get so much better for you, so don't you even dare think of doing anything stupid like me. You know, this might seem just like some sort a confessional early-in-the-morning sentiment. But listen. You'll always be that lovely junior house girl I took a liking to and smiled at and freaked out, and the loveliest person in the world. Basically, this is an apology of sorts for not being there with the whole ear-piercing fiasco, or for anything and for sometimes treating you like a child when I know full well you're not, and just to say. Take care of yourself. I love you, and I'll keep loving you, even when I'm not around.

Trisha.

General Provisions

If any beneficiary or beneficiaries of this Will shall contest the Will or in any manner attempt to have it or any trust or beneficial interest created by it declared invalid, such person or persons shall receive no benefits from or interests under this Will and my Will shall be carried out as if such person or persons had pre-deceased me.

I have entered neither into a contract to make wills nor into a contract not to revoke wills. Any similarity of the provisions of my Will to the provisions of the will of my witnesses or any other person, if any, executed on the same or on different dates than my Will, shall not be construed of as evidence of such a contract.

Unless specifically set forth in writing and acknowledged by the donee thereof, of any gift I have made or will make during my lifetime shall not be treated as satisfaction, in whole or in part, of any device or bequest in my Will.

On this 24th day of September, 2003, in the City of New York, State of New York, I hereby sign this document and declare it to be my last will.

In Memory of Trisha Low
(1988-2005)

Last Will & Testament of Trisha Low

I, Trisha Low of High Wycombe, Buckinghamshire, England, Great Britain declare that this is my Last Will & Testament.

Article I
Preliminary Declarations

Dear Mommy and Daddy,

Martha Braddell's brother killed himself today. He shot himself in the head. And I don't know why, but it hit me a lot less hard than a lot of other people in the room. I suppose it's because people here're just too sheltered. They've never written a suicide note, never thought about how they might do it, never hurt so badly they'd think they wanted to hurt themselves. In a way, I'm glad. This is the world. There are people who suffer all day in silence and would never tell anyone for fear of hurting any one else, until they're convinced that the only way to feel better would be to kill themselves, or hurt themselves, or. I don't know. I know I've felt that way before and I'll feel that way again it's was stupid, but it happens. This happens, and people feel this way, and somehow I'm glad people finally realise. And it hurts because somehow, I see all the damage I would have do if I were selfish, if I go through with it. If I ever cut too deep accidentally on purpose and take my own life. And I know how much all of this hurts you, and I'm sorry. I know how hard it's been to deal with me, and my not eating, and all those long sleeves in summer and keeping knives away and god I am really sorry. I know no suicide note would ever justify what I did to my family. It's terrible. There's no romanticism in suicide.

But here's the thing. I don't belong here, but I don't belong anywhere else. I'm treated as if I don't exist, yet everything revolves around me. I'd say 'I don't know what to do anymore!' but I do. I know what to do. And it's a toxic, disgusting thing to do but I need to. It's the only way.

So I guess, this is a not-suicide suicide note. This is a just-in-case note, because I'm weak, and I'm young, and stuff, and mostly I'm scared.

I love you, you know. I love the both of you. And I love Marsha. That's why it hurts so much to think about these things and worry about hurting you and then to feel guilty about it and then hurt again because it's hard to exist right now.

Everyone's saying that last night, when the news came around, that it felt like a dream. But I didn't have a dream last night so much as it seemed like a memory. And it's killing me to put it down here, but I guess if anything happens, I just want you to know that it is never because I didn't give you guys any consideration, or because I wanted to punish you, or because I was so blinded by sadness that I would forget how grateful I am to you both and how much I love you.

But you know, someone told me she was walking down the corridor and heard someone say 'yeah, Trisha Low's so scary, she's like, dead.' It seems almost inevitable.

Article II
Specific Bequests and Devises

In case anything happens, I know you guys will probably have to deal with all my stuff, so please make sure, for me, that the following people get the following things:

Charlotte: my necklace with the black crystal beading and all my Wong Kar Wai DVDs so

IN THE MOOD FOR LOVE
CHUNKING EXPRESS
2046

Tash: my illustrated Greek Myths and the following DVDs

MIRRORMASK
I <3 HUCKABEES
KILL BILL I and II
THUMBSUCKER
MOULIN ROUGE
R + J
BRICK
AMERICAN PSYCHO
MEAN GIRLS

Lottie: All of my Sinatra DVDs, all of my comics and whichever books she wants. All of my hats, my guitars (and my guitar polish and tuner) and the following DVDs

ZATOICHI
OLDBOY
SYMPATHY FOR LADY VENGEANCE
GREEN WING SEASON 1
EMPIRE RECORDS
ERASERHEAD
THE ELEPHANT MAN
CITY OF GOD
DELICATESSAN
PULP FICTION
BRICK

QUEER AS FOLK (SEASON 1)
HITCHCOCK (THE COMPLETE COLLECTION)

The following records and CDs

NINE INCH NAILS
ALL OF THE CURE (even though you hate them)
FRANZ FERDINAND
TORI AMOS
THE WHITE STRIPES
PEARL JAM (ugh, they were hers anyway)
RADIOHEAD
NO DOUBT
PLACEBO
THE SEX PISTOLS
DAVID BOWIE
IGGY POP

Laura: All of my Total Films, any of my books she wants.

Izzy: All of my Jeanette Winterson books.

Slaine: All of my Chuck Palahniuk and Amy Hempel
Marsha: literally whatever she wants, she is my little sister after all. She'll probably want all the rest of my jewellery.

Tor: My platform Mary Janes and Marilyn Manson hoodie

Edd: My ring with the heart and bat wings

I love you.
Trisha.

P.S. In case you need to get into anything.
Email password: dollcollector.
The key to my lockbox: underwear drawer–school dresser, top right.
UK bank account pin-code: 2189.
Locker combination: 65-47-22.

Article III
Executor and Administrative Powers

Dear Lottie

I guess this letter is more for thanks than it is for anything else. And you know, it's a just in case. First of all, thank you for being lovely and talking to me in all of my moments of complete and utter panic. Second of all I am very very sorry. I know I get unnecessarily stressed out by trivial things like work, and I know I shouldn't because it is not the most important thing in the world, but 13 years of thinking it is can take a toll on the way I see things.. So I'm sorry, but this is just in case. I just don't trust myself right now, and if something happened to me, or if I went crazy and did a stupid thing one night because of epic depression or something I just wouldn't forgive myself if I never got to say that. In some ways we're both too weak. You're too nice and I can't bear it, I don't deserve it and I don't know what I'd do without you. Remember when you said you'd get a:

tattoo of a vertebrae along your shoulderblades.

if you catch me on your tongue
and push my death-hair through your lungs
we'd all have lace-strangled necks
down-the-spine bolts and skin of the sun.
(not to get caught in the rib cage of the hour see)

Act One: The burial, in which hearts are stabbed through with needles and
strung on chains (they only cost a couple of hundred thousand)
But now they pay more for a deck of faded snap cards,
Yes, the kind we used to play in the common room, by the fire,
the very picture of domestic bliss, the very picture, the very picturesque
planning of murder lit by the fire; it made us red and gold and

ten

days

later

we:

painted the town in lurid colours,
blood and sunlight, the faded snap, the faded snap of twenty two necks—
but that only counts the dead, not the waiting, the to-be-dead,
the lumps of flesh and the sad awakening, they say :
Have you seen a boy, have you seen a man, really thin and dark? Have
you seen a dog, have you seen a Grim, have you seen something black?

The stars we used to wish upon lose their charm, morph into remnants of another's death rattle, the universe no longer has need for a creator. But this is a place where the sidewalk ends, and before the street begins. One day, we will look out the window and see that the moon has turned wine red; we will not stop to wonder, the glass will not reflect our awe. We will sit by the desk, fingers feverish through our hair, and ask ourselves 'Is this scientific phenomena?' wait hesitantly for physics to tell us what to think, and what no one will ask but this is an apocalypse and why aren't we ready to die?

(effigies are easier to burn)

I just want to be ready to die. It is almost unbearably cold, I slept with the window open and woke up feeling like someone had put ice cubes down my neck and behind my knees, and I couldn't feel my fingers. So I shut the window and sneaked into my old room across the hall, the one with the hot pipes running through it, and I'm sitting here as I'm writing this, in the corner with a pipe against my chin. The sun's coming up now, sort of, anyway, and I haven't done half the work I should have done, but I suppose it doesn't matter because it's tonight and who know what'll happen in an hour, or two, or more. Maybe because no one can define love, I can believe that it does exist. But I'm not sure I can wait long enough to find out.

And yet, I love you. I do.
Trisha

PS. Keep my diary away from my parents, will you. You know where it is.

Article IV
Guardianship Provisions

Dear Edd,

If, one day I am not here, suddenly and because of something we don't yet know.

Some things I remember:

I saw you yesterday; you made me tea (remembered I liked it white, two sugars)—the first thing you said was 'Look, I know technically we ended this—this us a long time ago, but I can't seem to forget, and I guess I wanted to see you,' and it confused me, but I missed you. I met your new girlfriend for the five minutes she was over and she seemed nice enough. Certainly pretty. We spent the day in on your bed talking, playing each other music, drinking schnapps; almost like the old days when we'd been just friends, nothing else, really. Before I left, you stroked my hair and said 'We've got to end this.' I reminded you we already had. You held me and played me a song that said everything you wanted to say, mouthed the words in my ear and kissed me softly when I teared up.

—and when I said 'You took my heart and he took my soul, but these things happen' it's not really true.

You can take my heart and soul because I'll let you.

Some things I remember:

We always leave large spaces of time between seeing each other, but it's almost ritual now. The way you pick me up and spin me round when you see me, laugh when I tell you to put me the fuck down. How I spend most of the night sitting in your lap, someone else's date, no less, fingers twined, smoking all of Iona's cigarettes.

You've lost weight again, but it's cold and you give me your jacket anyway, the wolf whistles from the girls who see me dismissed easily with a laugh and a quick 'He's just a friend.' We watch couples disappear into the garden one by one; this is leavers' ball after all, and chuckle as we almost get dragged into playing Circle of Fire. Rather, we chat about yaks and China and everything else that doesn't matter. Occasionally, I leave you for Freddie's lap and a gossip, or to hug the people who leave, but mostly it's more comfortable with you. Sentimentality is so bloody ridiculous.

When it's time to go, there's always a hug that lasts longer than necessary—you tangle your fingers in my hair when I hide my face in your jacket and we look at each other, cautious. But this time, your lips hover closer to mine and there's a split second where I think just maybe–just–but I'm the one who looks away first, and our half-sighs echo each other's as we pull away. The next time I'll see you is November, so I try not to watch your back as you go. Freddie catches my eye as I walk back in and hugs me properly. Not that there's any reason to. After all, you're just a friend.

The last thing I remember:
Remember when you said, you know how once you start believing someone can do no wrong, they can do no wrong?
And i said, you have no idea, babe.
I love you. Take care, darling, if you're reading this, I'm gone, and I probably already miss you.

Trisha.

Article V
Testamentary Trusts for Minor Child(ren)

to all of you at school:

this constant reinvention. yeah i was a different person when i woke up every day. but that never made me any less myself. it made me who i am because i wasn't ever tied down like you with all your grown up excuses for the way you act. i never made excuses because i didn't have to, and i won't now for what i've done. because the person you whose life you made utter hell yesterday wasn't ever me the next day. i feel sorry for you because you live like you do and you'll never live like i did, like the millions of people i've been. why live like you're afraid to be something else? you can say that i'm not being myself. or true to myself because i've done this now, taken it out on my wrist and left you all with no intention of ever coming back. You might even call me stupid, or crazy, or a coward. but the truth is that while i was here, i was more me than any of you will ever be. so go ahead and judge me, take your best shot cause even when i'm dead you'll never live like i did when i was alive.

trisha.

General Provisions

If any beneficiary or beneficiaries of this Will shall contest the Will or in any manner attempt to have it or any trust or beneficial interest created by it declared invalid, such person or persons shall receive no benefits from or interests under this Will and my Will shall be carried out as if such person or persons had pre-deceased me.

I have entered neither into a contract to make wills nor into a contract not to revoke wills. Any similarity of the provisions of my Will to the provisions of the will of my witnesses or any other person, if any, executed on the same or on different dates than my Will, shall not be construed of as evidence of such a contract.

Unless specifically set forth in writing and acknowledged by the donee thereof, of any gift I have made or will make during my lifetime shall not be treated as satisfaction, in whole or in part, of any device or bequest in my Will.

On this 6th June 2005, in the City of New York, State of New York, I hereby sign this document and declare it to be my last will.

**In Memory of Trisha Low
(1988-2007)**

Last Will & Testament of Trisha Low

I, Trisha Low of the City of Philadelphia, State of Pennsylvania, USA, declare that this is my Last Will & Testament.

Article I
Preliminary Declarations

Dear Mom and Dad,

It's been a crazy couple of years, but I guess in the end I've really grown up in many ways. Over my life I'm so grateful to have had so many people (some of which I hardly know) invite me into their lives and homes and take care of me. It is November and I am nineteen. Somehow, this year doesn't have the same romantic or depressing quality of last year, it's just very...tasteless. So, if you're reading this, it just got too bad, or too sad, or somehow, as they say, it all went south, and I'm sorry I'm gone.

Today was so pretty, one of those days where just by looking you couldn't tell if winter is just starting or it's ending and spring is coming round. Perfect time for leaving, I think, if one were to leave. I was thinking about how I'd be speechless about all of it if it did suddenly finally come to an end, because there's supposed to be only things to look forward to at this point. But maybe it's just that there is nothing romantic or depressing about this year at all, which means it's easy enough to walk away from everything. Two more weeks to go to thanksgiving, three weeks to winter time.

You know, the way that your body has learnt to cope with the air pressure from the atmosphere, all 101325 pascals, or 101325 newtons per meter squared of it, by pushing outwards, it would explode if you removed the air pressure, because your skin wouldn't be able to hold your insides in from the outward pushing. And there would be nothing pushing down on you to keep it in. Just like that I think we've learnt to cope with the feeling of growing older, not weekly or monthly or daily or secondly, but continuously and exponentially. Like compound interest. And that's why on your birthdays it doesn't feel like you're growing any older. It's just another day, the 234009348th day of your life, the 245893545th day. Once in a while there comes a point where it's been going on for so long that you can finally see the difference, you finally look at yourself and your life and you begin to feel old and the weight of your life dragging on the ground. You finally begin to feel your body pushing outwards and the pain of your skin beginning to break. But then, eventually, that's what our bodies have been made for. That's what they're supposed to do.

I've made some mistakes. This year, I don't think I've lost so many people in my life, but I've definitely lost. Relationships that will never be the same again. I guess I'm starting to realise what horrible things I've done to some people and how badly I've hurt some of them, including you but of course what is there to do now. People come and go, but who's to say that you should let them go? I don't fucking know what to do, really. Death, especially after all that highschool self destruction seems like it's become a trap that should have been over and done with, but somehow I can't shake the feeling that it's always coming and I'm not sure what's been holding it back.

Dear trap.
You are too beautiful;
Too beautiful for me.

In case it all gets too much, or in case the world decides, for me, that it's all quite enough. I've enclosed a bunch of other letters that I'd like you to give out to friends I love, and certain items that I'd like them to have. But let Marsha have what she wants first because I love her the most.

Thank you for everything. You mean so much, and I'm so grateful.

I love you.
Trisha.

PS. If you need to get into my email, the password is stayBeautiful1
My house/mailbox/bike/everything else keys should be in the dish on the counter by the door cause I guess I was always ready to leave.
The bank account numbers are in my wallet and in case you need it, my ATM PIN code is 2028 (UK and US)

Article II
Specific Bequests and Devises

Dear Lottie,

We haven't spoken in a while. I miss you. I feel like I've got to get out of here fast, everything is so large it doesn't feel like life. I'm drinking coffee because I can't drink a decent cup of tea. I want to smell the kinds of flowers I didn't realise I was smelling when I could, the little ones outside of the LAC at school, close to the smell of black leather schoolgirl shoes. America is dry, and yawning all the time. Even when people talk they sound like they're yawning. Everything is moist, and I miss the cold and dry, the time you told me, 'and I couldn't help but think of Sylvia Plath when you told me about how you put your face near the stove because it's been so long since you've felt the sun so near your skin'. I miss the not-sun and I miss you. And I'd hate to think of if something happened to me while I was gone and I never got to tell you I love you, even though it seems like there's not much left in the way of physical closeness to remember this love by.

Lottie, let me tell you a story.

Once upon a time, a girl read the wonder that is Norwegian Wood by Haruki Murakami. At around the same time, she stumbled upon, had, and lost a boy who reminded her so much of Nagasawa. She said to herself—he must read this book. She folded the corner down on page 31, which was a pageful of descriptions about him:

'When he asked someone to do something, the person would do it without protest. There was no choice in the matter.

'Nagasawa had a certain inborn quality that drew people to him and made them follow him. He knew how to stand at the head of the pack, to assess the situation, to give precise and tactful intstructions that others would obey. Above his head hung an aura that revealed his powers like an angel's halo, the mere sight of which would inspire awe in people for this superior being. Which is why it shocked everyone...

'There were sides to Nagasawa's personality that conflicted in the extreme. Even I would be moved by his kindness at times, but he could, just as easily, be malicious and cruel. He was both a spirit of amazing loftiness and an irredeemable man of the gutter. He could charge forward, the optimistic leader, even as his heart writhed in a swamp of loneliness. I saw these paradoxical qualities of his from the start, and I could never understand why they weren't just as obvious to everyone else. He lived in his own special hell.

'Still, I think I always managed to view him in the most favorable light. His greatest virtue was his honesty. Not only would he never lie, he would always acknowledge his shortcomings. He never tried to hide things that might embarrass him. And where I was concerned, he was unfailingly kind and supportive.'

And she lent the boy this book to read in the plane, because he would soon be taking a trip. She told him how there was a man in it who really reminded her of him, and to read it. The year came to an end, and passed. She never asked if he read it, or questioned if he saw the same similarities. She decided, he could have the book. After all, it was he who practically belonged in it anyway. They never spoke about it again.

Somewhere towards the end of the first third of the next year, the girl happened to be in a close–by thrift store that sold old things that people would donated, mostly for a personal need to get rid of things. She wasn't looking for anything in particular, but soon stumbled upon the bright purple and yellow cover of norwegian wood sticking out in the corner.

She picked it up and dusted it off, and checked for page 31, where the corner was folded down the exact same way. And then she bought back her heart for a dollar.

If you read this, then I want you to have that book. You'll find it because it's disguised among all the other books, looks just like the rest of them, but you'll know and I'll know, and he'll know, somewhere far away that it's not. You used to say that a secret shared is a secret doubled.

Thinking about it—this boy was less like Nagasawa than you are. Maybe in a different way, a quieter way that only I get to see or hear, but in that same way nonetheless. I want you to have it because you've been the most important person in my life, and if you're reading this, I guess it was short.

Here's to you, darling. Stay well, keep well, and enjoy that book. Because it'll mean you always know that you can give your heart away, but it'll come back round to you, dollar or no.

Love,
Trisha.

dear kaegan,

it's always kind of a great heart-warming moment when you find out that someone you had always believed would have, through no fault of their own, no time for you in the future, had always assumed that you'd know each other for the rest of your lives. i always thought that, even though now, if, you're reading this, i suppose that i'm gone, and we did, and time didn't prove the rule even if the proof is always in the pudding. know that i wanted to know you for the rest of my life, and you should have any of my books you want (especially the poetry ones), and a panda hat to prove it.

and, from the power and the glory by graham greene: '…his heart moved painfully, as when a man in love hears a stranger name a flower which is also the name of his woman.'

i feel like i've spent such a long time trying to be stuff that i'm nowhere near being able to touch and you're already there, already so much i want to be.

i thought a goodbye should be more ceremonious.
i tried to think of something that would be worthy of you,

but couldn't think of anything about from dousing this in whiskey and putting it in a petunia teacup inside of a cowboy boot and setting it all on fire. something like being incinerated. well, close to the heart, at least.

in the end i settled for leaving this in the drawer under all my underwear with the other letters but on top of all the other ones because your name is the prettiest and the most dangerous (not unlike yourself, sparks).

when i think of you, i think of loyalty because and it feels like it's been a really long time since i got here to america, damn, this place that seems all wrong, and you made it right for me, somehow. the strangest reason.

take care, i love you.
trisha.

Article III
Executor and Administrative Powers

dear grace—

if you're reading this, i'm gone. i want you to have all the american apparel you can find in my wardrobe. and all the skirts you want. and all the records you can carry (even if they're all in London). do whatever you will with that bike i was never able to ride properly.

wow, an ever so casual, gentle let down, grand finale, swan song.
no stupid new-age of this kind of education about love

so i just wanted to say
out of everything

remember the days when you said fuck the five o.
and life was carefree.
and life was good.

i love you.
trisha.

Article IV
Guardianship Provisions

dear nick,

i'm writing this at 1:45 am when i thought i would see you at 9, or at 3 am when i thought I would see you at 10, or at 9pm when i thought it would be 6. i'm writing this because i'm worried you got hit by a car, or are dead somewhere in a ditch, and by proxy i'm writing this because i'm worried tomorrow you'll be alive and i'll be hit by a car, somewhere with blood on my face and skirt hitched awkwardly against my thigh. somewhere not here where you won't even notice i'm gone. but if i am, and here you are, well, this is all i got. this is all i wanted to say. this is all i ever wanted.

like: if you're reading this it's like

SCENE lying on a bed next to you 1/2 drunk on 1/2 gin 1/2 lemonade and i'm gonna, i'm gonna, do everything i used to want to do. and i'm gonna, admit everything i used to feel.

sometimes i feel this really sick feeling, this heavy in my stomach like i'm going to lose something and i haven't figured out what it is, but it's probably definitely you and sometimes really means definitely all the time.

i'm scared that if i don't do something about it quick, everything's gonna be unsalvageable. but what do you do with that feeling? you can't act on it but you can't just put it away. it's like this irrational fear of giving someone your vulnerability, which is silly because if you're thinking it, you've already lost it. it's like when you want to do something really amazing, you want to give someone the love to end all loving, or something like that, but you know that as many times as you say, tonight's going to be the night, it'll never happen, it'll never work out, it's just this stupid ideal. and you know deep down that life is about losing things as well. and one of the biggest mistakes is, just knowing someone is very different from saying wait right there, i have some love to give. lying in bed is a useless way of dealing with this feeling, and sitting around in your room waiting for someone to turn up is no way to get close. it's about taking risks and saying, shhh, right now i don't know how you feel, but here, this is what i feel, and that's all right, everything's all right. and, it's like how you feel you should ignore someone even if you want them really badly because that's the only way of dealing with it. i guess sometimes it makes me happy just to stop and look, because watching someone you love just going about their way and interacting with other people without your interrupting can be a pretty beautiful thing. i was talking to someone a long time ago about how you come to understand that it's really about giving someone what's important to them instead of giving someone what's important to you because they become so important to you. that their happiness becomes what you want as well. and, i think what you come to understand is, it's a feeling that you're losing something but then you realise from all movies you've ever seen; you can't lose something you never had.

there are people that definitely shouldn't be messed with, people who just pretend; there are ones that aren't healthy to be around for too long. the kind i just go to pretty helplessly. the pretty ones. nice voices. good harmonies. leather jackets. slim wrists. considered poses. old-young men. soft spots. people who want to cling onto around their bodies. seems like i have a lot of those dreams nowadays. you're one of them. you're all of them. i love you.

people tell me that it's hard to believe but you kind of used to be a real person. you know? i fell in love with you and now you've broken my heart. but if you're not whole, then maybe that's what's wrong here because that's all i got, that's all i fell in love with, what's left over of you. but you can't love something that won't let itself see how it's broken.

'you're sad.'
'what? no, i'm not.'
'no, i can tell. you smell different.'

and now i'll say, maybe this half and hour, this whatever we had, was enough. actually, because who wants a 24/7, that's boring. and now i'll say you had me at hello. what can i do. and i'm just gonna wake up tomorrow and it'll fade every time i wake up, or maybe, if you're reading this i won't even wake up at all.

but then at least you'll know.
but then at least i'll be glad i had this moment. the end.

Trisha.

General Provisions

If any beneficiary or beneficiaries of this Will shall contest the Will or in any manner attempt to have it or any trust or beneficial interest created by it declared invalid, such person or persons shall receive no benefits from or interests under this Will and my Will shall be carried out as if such person or persons had pre-deceased me.

I have entered neither into a contract to make wills nor into a contract not to revoke wills. Any similarity of the provisions of my Will to the provisions of the will of my witnesses or any other person, if any, executed on the same or on different dates than my Will, shall not be construed of as evidence of such a contract.

Unless specifically set forth in writing and acknowledged by the donee thereof, of any gift I have made or will make during my lifetime shall not be treated as satisfaction, in whole or in part, of any device or bequest in my Will.

On this 11th November, 2007, in the City of New York, State of New York, I hereby sign this document and declare it to be my last will.

In Memory of Trisha Low
(1988-2008)

Last Will & Testament of Trisha Low

I, Trisha Low of the City of Philadelphia, State of Pennsylvania, USA, declare that this is my Last Will & Testament.

Article I
Preliminary Declarations

Dear Mom and Dad,

I have this whole thing right now about how I'm finding America really lovely nowadays.

I had one of those life-defining moments on AIM last night. Sounds shallow when i say it like this but it's true.

I want to cry cause no one knows what they're doing here
no one can just do nothing and not feel guilty
no one can talk like whimsical happy people
no one will just let go and let's just play
no one's going to whisk me away to a daydream world
no one can talk like a dream.
no one's going to carry me on their back
no one's going to cry for me.
there's no one to sing to or sing for,
no one going to tell me, 'you're the one.'
and come away with me to a daydream
and no one's gonna have to cry.

And then you realise how things go on, you wake up in the morning and can't get out of bed, it's warmer than it's been for months, the sun shines a warm glow, almost misty, to everything, a boy and a girl are wearing flowers in their hair from the fairytale meadow near the man-made dam. The temperature gets higher 10 degrees every hour, then subsides. Sky gets dimmer so unnoticeably now everything's in this lovely rainy state. The sky's way too bright for 8pm, even with daylight savings, and that's how you can tell spring is here. Bright but overcast with high-contrast clouds, drizzling slightly and the sky's this even shade of blue after a few minutes, the trees still burnt into the sky. I have a moment like that and all it does is make me wonder how in thirty seconds it could be gone. And just in case it is, in case I leave suddenly, in case I decide on another night like this that it's a good way to be gone:

I'm too emotional when it comes to shootings and countdowns, oh well.

It's been a while since I locked my fingers and closed my eyes and pretended to pray. I just want to hold somebody's hand.

It seems like I can't do that while I'm here.

It strikes me how little you know about me since I moved here, that I drink coffee, black and sweet, and that my fingers smell like cigarettes and my calves are kissed often with bike grease, my arms with bruises. That I've known love and lost it, that I've grown out of the smell of mothballs and oiled razors into the smell of leather around my neck or my wrists, that all I want is for it to be warm, clear and dark—lying on the library green wearing as little as possible. But if you get this, maybe this is how you should remember me, even if you never saw it, or even if you're surprised and upset with the blood and the BDSM and the sex, because it's lovely. And you should feel that if I'm gone, I went when I was young, and stupid and hopeful, even if the way I feel and the way I acted never seemed that way.

I am hyper-aware. I need to stop. it is like being poked with pins when all i want to do is sit quietly and be a stuffed animal. I want things, everything nowadays comes down to my wanting things. But i guess that's how things should be? I worry too much about what other people want and it is quite nice to say, yes, although yes has always been the easiest word for me, for better or for worse.

You see, I'm sick of the 'when you get there's'

I'm quite sick of keeping myself in check for that, when you never get there, not really. Always something else.

Maybe it's the something else that was always more important.

Like, tell Marsha that the most important thing I ever learned was to never underestimate the power of a great haircut at a crucial moment.

Someone told me once, that things become very poorly colourised.

I love you,
Trisha.

PS. If you need to get into my email, the password is stayBeautiful1
My house/mailbox/bike/everything else keys should be in the dish on the coffee table by the door
The bank account numbers are in my wallet and in case you need it, my ATM PIN code is 2028 (UK and US)

Article II
Specific Bequests and Devises

dear kaegan,

it's that point at the very tip of summer where life seems at the point of dying again.
running away is never going to be the way to find whatever i'm looking for. or whatever bullshit. bff
means you get my second/third/fourth thoughts: i want to make it wonderful and happy and i'm trying. i really do.

i actually realised something: quite a while ago. i'm never going to find anything if it's not even something to find but it's something that's wrong with me. which means i'm never going to be able to run
away from it. but i'm too tired to change. and it kills me most at times like this.

when i think of you i think about two dresses and one scent.

it's been tough recently for us both and i know you would just probably tell me to be sensible get my
shit together. instead, i have an urge to say something about a beautiful night and perfect things, but
what is the point when i'm stuck in this room.

the point tonight is that you are beautiful and brilliant and no one should be able to take that away
from you, even with the sort of careless accident like 'would you hold my hand' and boys that kiss
you too far down the supermarket aisle. a bag of frozen peas and a pack of cigarettes.

this is just in case something terrible happens and i don't get to tell you any of this in person any
more, or ever. but even when i'm gone, remember, at the same time as we're declaring a war, we
can never really declare a war, and that's what's so wonderful/awful about being a girl.

i want you to keep the books you want, especially that copy jack spicer's admonitions i've marked
up—that one i want you to have, and make sure james gets that copy of my o'hara, and maybe share
the waldrops between each other. after that, make sure everyone else gets their pick, i couldn't bear
to think all of my books being put in storage somewhere, no touching, no trace, etc.

i love you, take care.
trisha

dear nick,
it was this conversation during english once, a long time ago.

'pick a sentence to start off with.'
'i'm not in love with you.'

[...]

ARKHAM ASYLUM

XD -7764

CONFIDENTIAL

TRANSCRIPT: PATIENT INTERVIEW

1) ON FORM 404 PRINT YOUR NAME AND THE DATES ON WHICH YOU HAD ACCESS TO THE DOCUMENT(s)

2) TO AVOID UNAUTHORIZED DISCLOSURE, AT NO TIME SHOULD THE DOCUMENT(s) BE LEFT UNATTENDED.

3) THE DOCUMENT(s) ARE TO BE TRANSPORTED TO PERSONS WITH THE NECESSARY SECURITY CLEARANCE.

4) RECEIVE A VOUCHER AFTER RELEASING THE DOCUMENT(s).

IMPORTANT: PLEASE KEEP THIS VOUCHER FOR YOUR RECORDS

CONFIDENTIAL INFORMATION (PAGE 7 OF 28)

Patient Interviews:
Patient Interview #1, March 21st

HARLEY QUINN: Patient interview number 1.

JOKER: So, I'm your first, am I, toots? You know what they say, you never forget your first time. I'll try to make it memorable for you.

HARLEY QUINN: Oh, you already have. Tell me, why do you do the things you do?

JOKER: Why do you think I do it?

HARLEY QUINN: Fame, notoriety, a desire to stand out from the crowd? A wicked sense of humor.

JOKER: (Gasp) You're good! How did you figure me out, Doc? I've had doctors poking around in here for years and no one was as astute, and if you don't mind my saying, beautiful as you.

HARLEY QUINN: Really? Oh, you're just playing with me.

JOKER: Well, you'll never know, will you, unless...

HARLEY QUINN: Unless what? Tell me!

CONFIDENTIAL INFORMATION (PAGE 12 OF 28)

Patient Interviews:
Visitor #11, April 19th

JOKER: I'm the joker. I do things that are funny, Bats. What's funny about watching an innocent girl die?

BATMAN: That doesn't match your M.O. and you know it.

JOKER: So what if I do or don't? What do you really want to know? Tell me and I'll bite.

BATMAN: Enough! Where will the next target be?

JOKER: You're really too easy to fire up. It isn't a question of where, darling, more of a 'who' question, dontcha know.

BATMAN: Talk.

JOKER: It's

DOCUMENT ENDS HERE

Patient Interviews:
Appendix A, Police Radio Scanner, April 22nd

HARLEY QUINN: End of the line, Puddin'!

HARLEY QUINN: I loved you but you never cared! All you did was hurt me, throw me away and laugh at me!

HARLEY QUINN: Now I'm gonna to the same to you!

JOKER: Would it help if I said I was sorry?

HARLEY QUINN: <3 YEAH! <3

[...]

if you read this, i'm gone, and i know all i need to know, baby. i'm not in love with you. take my comics—you know where they are—and the copy of Please Kill Me with the inscription that reminds me how i liked when you called me kitten.

never forget[it's a joke].

trisha.

Article III
Executor and Administrative Powers

dear cecilia

i have such a big problem with facing stuff, so i guess it's unsurprising that i worry how someday i might give up and just be gone. from this point here this will be kind of senseless but it's just stuff i don't want to forget. //

a play on texture, threaded through with red, sectioned eyes. carved out. stained red the hands and whitish bleached wax—like look to the rest of it. it's kind of a response to plato's symposium about people being pregnant, plus androgyny by garbage about getting harder. the idea is basically about girls with erections. the top part sweeping away into darkest blue like heavenly. the lesbians called her marvin gaye. but we knew her as malena like the movie. well i think _____ is the kind of guy who's confident enough to know how attractive he is that he doesn't have to fish for compliments. and i guess that's pretty effing sexy. we do pretty well. sacred space: representation of negative space, mystery, reminiscent of, the curve of the head in the womb, the most natural basic thing i could think of anyway, random, orifices? lips, that sculpture in a clockwork orange, a friend said so what you're doing is really suggestive fruits, but it's not about that. a built—in pedestal (which is part of it not attached because of the purist—thing, and hopefully something symbolic.) contrast that divine/religion thing >/= the conceptual writing thing, hopefully by this year, stuff like reminding each other to PROTECT THE WILDFLOWERS. I'm up to 15 and you're at 22 and it depends. these love-hate relationship with boys that mean 'it wasn't my bullet' and how it doesn't matter when we've got nothing to say to each other apart from 'haha' and we smile. this huge big debate about ciga-rettes until five am in the morning, while my nose is bleeding like crazy. i could be dead today. i got this ticket anyway, and a bag with no luggage in it so to speak.

keep the bataille and simone weil, and the hogarth so you can remember me with the emptiness behind the femininity of his serpentine line, scooped out spaces for male imaginations.

i love you,
trisha.

Article IV
Guardianship Provisions

dear thomson,

just in case i never got to tell you in person:

'i like you.'

'why?'

'you want to fight.'

'the world is my boxing ring.'

'do you have to fight everyone?'

'only the enemy.'

'is it that simple?'

'you can be so subtle you just tie yourself up in knots.'

'you can be so simple you just go nine rounds with yourself.'

'well yes, i do, often.'

'what for?'

'to stay on my toes.'

'you should relax.'

'i look silly in an armchair.'

'what do you look like in bed?'

and now you know (all the trouble i would have caused). i wish i coulda watched some scenes of extreme violence […] with you. i remember well, i guess there was this strange, awkward attraction that made us sit next to each other and not quite want to mess things up by speaking. one day i'll knock on your door, and you'll say, we can do this. i had this dream two days ago where we touched our mouths together and didn't move at all.

trisha.

Article V
Testamentary Trusts for Minor Child(ren)

the most beautiful // terrifying thing everyone should ever remember:

'it was nice to know
that when i was
watching you secretly,
that you were watching
me too.' DRAFT 10:19pm AUG 7

i love you all,
trisha.

General Provisions

If any beneficiary or beneficiaries of this Will shall contest the Will or in any manner attempt to have it or any trust or beneficial interest created by it declared invalid, such person or persons shall receive no benefits from or interests under this Will and my Will shall be carried out as if such person or persons had pre-deceased me.

I have entered neither into a contract to make wills nor into a contract not to revoke wills. Any similarity of the provisions of my Will to the provisions of the will of my witnesses or any other person, if any, executed on the same or on different dates than my Will, shall not be construed of as evidence of such a contract.

Unless specifically set forth in writing and acknowledged by the donee thereof, of any gift I have made or will make during my lifetime shall not be treated as satisfaction, in whole or in part, of any device or bequest in my Will.

On this 9th August, 2008, in the City of New York, State of New York, I hereby sign this document and declare it to be my last will.

In Memory of Trisha Low
(1988-2009)

Last Will & Testament of Trisha Low

I, Trisha Low of the City of Philadelphia, State of Pennsylvania, USA, declare that this is my Last Will & Testament.

Article I
Preliminary Declarations

dear mom and dad,

i'm afraid this isn't going to be a very interesting letter. it might even border on scary. i would like to pretend like i'm doing well, but i don't really have it in me to front. you're probably not even going to get this letter, but i can't really tell anyone else this stuff, let alone you guys in 'real life' i guess, because everyone's just as stressed out as i am, or more emotionally traumatised, and it's rubbing off a little, if anything. if you're reading this, then somehow i'm gone—maybe something awful happened or maybe one day i broke, or someone broke me, but this is just in case—maybe so you'll have some answers, or explanations, or maybe you could even just imagine a little bit of what my life has been since i'm so often so far away.

damn. i'm tired, i can't sleep (and i've tried everything). I've taken to making assorted baked goods and custards in the dead of night and giving them away for brunch in the mornings. i take a shower at two am and then i laugh hysterically at myself because my next thought is usually something like 'maybe i'll make crumb cake. maybe gabe will want some to take to school tomorrow.' i've turned into a parody of myself, and it feels a little raw around the edges, like when my lipstick has blurred and that couple of milimeters of colour changes me from 'put together' to 'crazy, possibly a slut.' i don't know, things are going well work-wise. tonight i will probably make tapioca cake. maybe i will finally figure out how to make a perfect sixty degree egg. i'm tired of having to talk to other people about their lives—i'm tired of talking about all that. man, even hal freaked out the other day and she's the calmest most evolved human out of anyone i know. show me the drugs already, anything that'll get me to sleep.

i've been having strange dreams, but not bad ones; between the magpies scrabbling beneath my skin to find some microscopic treasure and infant beauty pageants and being stabbed in the belly by a clan somewhere between the westboro baptist church and a group of hairy biker men,

i walked to work really wanting to listen to iggy pop, so i did. street-walking cheetah/with a heart full of napalm and all—i never understood why that's always been the canonical iggy pop lyric, but recently, thinking about entrance wounds/text/no exits, fragments and glass growing arduously through performative skins, perhaps things are coming to a head and i should just sit down and write something. searching and destroying always seemed mindless to me, and searching-to-destroy such a masculine sentiment. searching is destroying, already, maybe, who knows.

'to study the way with the body means to study the way with your own body. It is the study of the way using this lump of red flesh. Everything which comes forth from the study of the way is the true human body. […] The coming and going of birth and death is the true human body.'

my piece on BDSM went up on carnal nation today, which i could barely believe—and i guess if you're reading this i know you'll end up finding out some things about me that you might not understand, or want to understand—things like swapping out razors for other kinds of bruises and going to work at a place where there's bad industrial music, too-young girls giggling at men with scary eyes and a lot of money under the table. i guess i never really had a bad experience there, but never a good one either—i always just felt compelled to go, like it would make me older or wiser, or at least teach me something about someone i didn't particularly care for, and if not then being paid to try felt good. someone's little fetish toy for an hour or so. A denial of one's own 'real' body for a dream is also to open yourself up to an intense awareness of the emptiness of a flesh-core.
'in themselves, no. each one of them is a mirror, dedicated to the person that I particularly want to look into it. but mirrors can be arranged. the frightening hall of mirrors in a fun house is universal beyond each particular reflection.' it is not about making mirrors, for me, or bringing people to them, it is to refract into vitrious membranes (and so the maze becomes a labyrinth, warped and unpredictable, but escape never crosses the mind).

'she'll be losing her mind to a tricky voice and a full moon, and like as not, i'll be saddled with the consequences.'

i have been reading a lot of badly written detective fiction—i like the idea of a macguffin, this absent thing, this weird hole that entire plots are constructed around, when it is barely a glimmer, and because of it, stories falter and firmer surfaces give way. things resolve upwards, not downwards into some kind of interior, some kind of core (value). 'first, you find a little thread, the little thread leads you to a string, and the string leads you to a rope, and from the rope you hang by the neck. what kind of a girl was she, this friend of yours.' but the implications of this stretch beyond the theory of gravity all the characters maintain—instead, steamy dissipations. One absurd logic debunking another, exhuming stories from a hybridised flesh. the thing about noir is, everyone is a fugitive from the laughing house and the ashtrays are always full.

i've been thinking a lot about old friends and how much i've changed—some of them probably wouldn't recognise me. but hey, i'm not sure i'd like them too. i like my different worlds, but it's good for them to scrape at each other once in a while. i guess i've moved around a bunch and it's always this sense of feeling like a ghost-person before i decide i want to walk on the ground instead of just above it and anchor yourself in something, someplace, for me, usually someone.

it feels like the world is going to swallow me whole.

if you're reading this, i just wanted to say—i'm sorry if anything i ever did ever hurt you. i'm sorry if i'm so selfish so often. i'm so grateful for everything you've done for me. i really am. and never doubt that i loved you because i did, maybe more than i ever let you know.

Trisha.

PS. If you need to get into my email, the password is stayBeautiful

My house/mailbox/bike/everything else keys should be in the dish on the coffee table by the door
The bank account numbers are in my wallet and in case you need it, my ATM PIN code is 2028 (UK and US)

Article II
Specific Bequests and Devises

dear kaegan,

i am writing this to you nestled in my duvet, 'flailing around in my bed,' as you say. you're at the gym, i think.

how scary, right, that the now you isn't the old you. that we've known each other so long now.

i guess when I think of you i think of best friendship, which means no one can tell you the facts of your own life (definitely not yourself), but to tell the story over is the only way you can make it material. so like a virus in the sense of watching it dance about the surface of some digitised skin—like television.

which I guess is also to say In The Commonwealth nothing is a fact unless you've checked it thrice, which means, your life is not a fact, and neither is mine. there are pictorial ideas//ideals mirroring into our narrative. maybe we're just all feeding back into the same idea of 'character development.' something that at the same time affirms the ability of stereotypical mode to give significant meaning to a truth. a cliché is a fact in any given world/character and yet at the same time is an utter failure, an impossible staging. and yet, these images used, they are recognised, a beckoning.

look, they fell for it,

i don't know why i keep writing these 'just in case' letters unless that i guess now or maybe it's all just an elaborate personal joke, but if you're getting this you'll probably understand.

when i think about you darling, it's as intimate as doing my laundry because you've known more iterations of me than anyone else. thinking about barging into each other's rooms, moving in tandem in the kitchen because i owe so many parts of myself to you. but we're not twins either because if i move my fingers the same way you do, it doesn't mean people will see it the same way. if i smile it doesn't mean i'll be as happy as you are or vice versa. friends like you create a tesseract that get you from point a to point b by disguising point a. between you and me, there's a vagrant contingency. it's weaving together at the same time as weaving away. kaegan this letter got kind of messy but darling, i don't even know, because i mean, what even is the way to enter the form of our lives?

if you get this, it means i'm gone, and I want you to know how special you are to me, and how much i wouldn't have done without you. in other words, yes. in other words, the are same point twice. this is also a way of showing how the point isn't singularly valid to begin with. 'i can see it, so it's like i can.' if you get this, i want you to have all of my jack spicer, especially that marked up copy of admo-nitions. i love you, take care.

trisha.

Article III
Executor and Administrative Powers

dear cecilia,

let's play dress up.

TL: Remember the first time I met you? It was in London at Maureen Paley. You were setting up your black drumkit and I was dragging out my black drumkit… I was thinking 'Oops! What's the look on his face going to be as I'm dragging out my black drumkit versus his black drumkit!'

CKC: I had a black metal band from Norway there. So it was sort of like, 'okay, well, I've got the validation of the scary people who kill people.'

TL: Right. And I had no validation.

CKC: You didn't have any freaky long-haired murderers.

TL: Game match. No, let's just admit that we're hopeless romantics. The first time you struck a chord in me was in Basel when we were walking past that bridge by the river, looking at the moon and at the moonlight in the river. I said something about how it was romantic and you said, 'That's exactly what the idea of romance is.' I answered that you meant it was the idea of us wanting to jump off the bridge: that's romanticism, because it would be beautiful.

CKC: Romanticism is predicated on failure. You know what are the leitmotifs in the Romantic canon in its strict classical sense? Goethe's The Sorrows of Young Werther is about suicide…and Caspar David Friedrich—Oh! It's a ruined church. It's a shipwreck.

TL: Wanting to destroy yourself 'cause you put yourself in that ship.

CKC: It's not even that. You love something so much to the point that you will allow for it to scare you and become more total.

TL: You want something so much that you actually see it. All the narratives that I use aren't about violence. That's not the subject. The violence is proof of belief but whatever For instance, during my show at the Whitney in 2005, Snorre Ruch [black metal musician], who was involved in murders and church burnings, elaborated a fantasy that created a system of belief that people couldn't dis-engage from. He was the better artist in that show.

and our throats were bare for god.

remember to always be careful with each other so you can be dangerous together. if you get this, i'm gone, but my old copy of *brideshead revisited* is yours—'o god, make me good, but not yet.'

love,
trisha.

Article IV
Guardianship Provisions

dear thomson,

today i pricked my finger, but i can't remember when there was a wheel. there was coffee too, though, so that was okay. if you're reading this i'm gone, and if you're reading this, this is how I feel—

[…]

your room nowadays feels more touchingly real to me than my own. sharpness of the words on your wall, a hard pillow, segments of waterstained ceiling. i sit crosslegged on your silly printed couch, you speak, and i like that i have no power over your voice—we could be in different rooms, i could stuff my ears with static, and it'd probably still round the corners and run its way through me, make my blood rise. perhaps it's because i'm so used to my own silences (of which there are many), but the reverberations run sharper that i'm used to and trying to shed them only spreads the charge. it reminds me that a girl needs her own room because sometimes she needs to sleep naked in sheets that are so clean they're cold, lick the salt off her cheeks and reconcile herself to her own image. but after that, it becomes easier to see dualities.

[…]

these are suspect places.

[…]

more than anything (even more than daddy longlegs and rotten eggs) i am afraid of violating the terms of this agreement, but i've lost the sheet of paper i printed out and signed, i can't even remember who i made it with (it could have been me?). my experience tells me that the warning signals are insidious; there are no alarms.

[…]

2.
The skin-sack
In which wanton duality
Packed
All the completions

Of my infructuous impulses
Something the shape of a man
To the casual vulgarity of the merely observant
More of a clock-work mechanism
Running down against time
To which I am not paced

My fingertips are numb
from fretting your hair
A God's doormat
On the threshold of your mind.

3.
We might have coupled
In the bedridden monopoly of a moment
Or broken flesh with one another
At the profane communion table
Where wine is spilled on promiscuous lips

We might have given birth to a butterfly
With the daily news
Printed in blood on its wings

– Mina Loy, *Love Songs to Joannes.*

[…]

i have become socialised to sometimes think of my life as some kind of high school movie, with people, colours and words clearly delineated, hierarchies strictly defined. it's the strange need of wanting to know where one stands, if one does at all (and of course, really we should all lay down and drink some warm milk). it is why i like the intersubjectivities of theory that reads like an open wound, it's a remedy of sorts. abstractly, in my mind (and you're not going to like this one bit), you're the jock who still aces school and i'm the weird girl who stays overtime in the art studio because she likes that the teacher wants in her pants. but somehow we've ended up here, you're brash and funny and i'm quiet and austere, we're opposite signs, and i don't know what to think of this crook-edness. sometimes i get that feeling like before you vault over a bar and you know you're going to hit it because you can't quite reach as high as the person before (or maybe you're just short, ha ha), and then i have to remind myself that this bar doesn't actually exist. certainly, though, (and we're back to real life now), when we're together i feel like we're unsutured, languidly half-stitched and it feels damned fine.

[…]

i wonder if you remember that time we were in bed and you were drunk, and we'd fucked and you asked me if i knew if you were in love with me. i said yeah and kissed you and told you i loved you too, which i don't think really answered the question. i promised myself minutes ago that this wouldn't be a love letter, but now these words have become like spasms, involuntary and mutating.

love,
trisha.

dear thomson,

if you're reading this, i'm gone, but i'm so quiet that there's still things i want to say, so i guess i'll say them here. i think that this letter is honest and that i haven't hidden things in folds and different kinds of 'I's like i usually do. this letter is just me like i am right now.

on love & fear (or maybe they're the same).

i've suppose i've never dated a boy who didn't know exactly how to make me cry. you might not know it, but you do. know how, that is. exactly. i don't know what exactly that says about me. i don't know a lot of things right now, and i think the world is telling me it's a state i should get used to; that letting things sit and stew might just be something i have to get used to. i learnt to make things move because i hated the way things were in my life, and now when i get scared, i have to move, otherwise i feel like i'm going to die, or it's going to stick, or worse, still, that it means there's nothing i can do to make it feel better. usually i move into the scared—feeling but sometimes doing that is more like rash, heastrong, suicide like a running away. i guess i cry all the time anyway, so i'm not really sure if that's a thing that matters any more.

i remember a long time ago, when we first started sleeping together and i told kirsten, way before we even talked about being together past twisting loosely as lovers, or desiring from afar, that you'd probably break my heart. i said 'he doesn't even know it yet, but he will and i'm not sure he's ever had his heart broken. that scares me.' have you ever had your heart broken? maybe not. it's something that instills a great sense of dread, and it colours everything that happens afterwards in an endless, linear, slow motion. and i hate linearity. it bores everyone. it changes colours, and you can't really remember what it was like before.

thomson, i've had my heart broken before, not in the sudden, awful way that people think is how it happens, or how people think it's the worst, but in the way where there's a fork, and maybe a bird and it's slow and long, and by the time you feel a slight, short pang, it's too late for any of the shreds to be sutured back together.

'there was no person such as marilyn monroe [...] invented like an author creates a character'

it is unclear who is the author and who is the character. i wonder if she wrote herself through her experiences with others. i wonder if i do. after all, people, they do that with their two faces, and one can be helped, and one can't.

[...]

i wrote this a long time ago. i fancied myself much more after rosmarie waldrop, then.
you kissed me under the statue of st. catherine of alexandria and the wheel started to spin. i wrote my lips under your palm because i fancy myself impulsive—pricked my finger long before your touch led my wrist. but things for me begin at the reeling of pronouns and you were certain that my I was not an eye, it stood alone. so there it was, the hitching of skirts before the reining in of an I-love-you. a golden calf, a bloodless sacrifice.

[...]

'a swirl of drugs and bad men, and her wrecked sense of self.'

[...]

there was a great moment, sometime last year, when kirsten had just broken up with michael tom (or maybe it was two years ago), and her and grace kidnapped me and brought me to a little restaurant called chloe for my birthday dinner. i had steak, because i like meat and i have no guilts, having seen several kinds of animals slaughtered before, and have slaughtered a number of kinds of seafood myself.

kirsten said she knew she hadn't been in love with michael tom. she asked 'what's it like, being in love.'

grace and i answered, immediately 'well, mostly it's awful.' we didn't even have to look at each other.

[...]

people ask all the time, well do you love this person? do they love you? but what does that really mean? the way people see it is that its this essential force that can't be stopped if it exists. a kind of love that is always correct, a kind of veto, or trump card. and so there can be a universally wrong way to do it.

no. the question that should be asked is 'do you love *how* they love you'.

there's not right or wrong, there's just doing. and it feels or it doesn't.

do you love how they can take you over, or do you feel like it's an alien invasion that needs to be stopped (with just 24 hours in which to do so.)

[...]

this section is called what if, which is also a kind of armour.

the risky thing about open relationships is that it feels, always, like a puzzle that needs one last piece—but there are two left and neither of them exactly fits.

that, however, is not the reality of the situation. it just makes it easier to think about it that way. easy is cheating.

i'm the kind of girl who doesn't believe she deserves anything unless she's had to break in some way to get it. and if i haven't, then perhaps it's not real. but then again, i don't believe someone who won't break to get something that they think they want either. wanting is empty unless there is work. work, and risk.

i've gotten better about thinking this stuff (it's epically unhealthy), but the rhetoric seems somehow embedded in how feelings come up in my throat. and then i choke.

what if.

[…]

how hard can you break me? very hard, i think.

that's what i remembered, after this weekend.

i am skittish because frankly, i'm bendy, but i don't know how many breaks i have left in me. i've lived through a few.

i suddenly realise that i'd forgotten that trust was even a thing, until recently. which is remarkable, because it's always been a Big One for me. i forgot about trust, and then i lost some of it, i think, and there it is, visible again, a buckling black bind.

and at the end of the day, i don't like thinking that someone apart from myself could be responsible for the way, or ease with which i crack, or fracture. it's all my fault.

isn't it?

[…]

i love you. i don't think i've ever loved someone more.

[…]

wherever i am as you read this—i probably miss you already. yeah, cause regardless, i think you're extraordinary magic.

[…]

'this is the most important letter you will ever receive.'

love,
trisha.

General Provisions

If any beneficiary or beneficiaries of this Will shall contest the Will or in any manner attempt to have it or any trust or beneficial interest created by it declared invalid, such person or persons shall receive no benefits from or interests under this Will and my Will shall be carried out as if such person or persons had pre-deceased me.

I have entered neither into a contract to make wills nor into a contract not to revoke wills. Any similarity of the provisions of my Will to the provisions of the will of my witnesses or any other person, if any, executed on the same or on different dates than my Will, shall not be construed of as evidence of such a contract.

Unless specifically set forth in writing and acknowledged by the donee thereof, of any gift I have made or will make during my lifetime shall not be treated as satisfaction, in whole or in part, of any device or bequest in my Will.

On this 30th May, 2009, in the City of New York, State of New York, I hereby sign this document and declare it to be my last will.

In Memory of Trisha Low
(1988-2011)

Last Will & Testament of Trisha Low

I, Trisha Low of the City of New York, State of New York, USA, declare that this is my Last Will & Testament.

Article I
Preliminary Declarations

dear mom and dad,

guess i'm trying pretty hard to remove this nicotine chokehold on my lungs because one day i'm just going to end up naked facedown on some bear rug and i'll have some fucked up dream about something someone said about me on the internet. i don't know what attaches me so strongly to the idea of smoking, it's the kind of romanticism that's actually kind of trite, like a counterfeit, or the kind of decoupage people the nouveau riche had in their parlours at the end of the nineteenth century. the kind of romanticism like how people say the sea is constantly jerking off//into itself//like we're all just jerking off all the time. all i want, i think, is to interfere with my own ability to deal with adult concerns, like doing 'something' with my life, or dying or something, instead of propagating—i'm going to take this little moment to lovingly toughen up one of the nails digging into the lid of some not-yet-existent coffin. i guess if you're reading this i'm like really, actually gone—and i'm sorry, and i probably miss you guys already—

because, i guess, or but, you know, at this point i'm tired of explaining myself—i'm sure you'll find out some things about me, and that i've written that you're going to hate. i know you guys love me even though it might be difficult to love me for who i am right now, but i guess i just want you to know that i never meant to hurt you guys, or to make you unhappy. i love you so much and i'm so incredibly grateful for everything you've done for me. i guess just—

'but people can't, unhappily, invent their mooring posts, their lovers and their friends, anymore than they can invent their parents. life gives these and also takes them away and the great difficulty is to say yes to life […] people are too various to be treated so lightly. I am too various to be trusted.' – James Baldwin, *Giovanni's Room*.

i love you, and i just want you to know, that whatever you find out, it was mostly a way of saying yes, rather than saying no.

Trisha.

PS. if you need to get into my email, the password is stayBeautiful1
my house/mailbox/bike/everything else keys should be in the dish on the coffee table by the door
the bank account numbers are in my wallet and in case you need it, my ATM PIN code is 2028 (UK and US)

Article II
Specific Bequests and Devises

to everyone i love,

if you're reading this i guess i've already left. i remember once someone asked me if they had kept me waiting cause that's what everyone wants to hear. and i said no, i had already left because no wants to be kept waiting.

'she is the one person i know who is literally a chainsmoker. she lights each one from the butt of the last; how she lights the first one of the day remains to me a mystery, for she never seems to have any matches in the house when i ask her for one. i once arrived to find her in great distress because her current cigarette has fallen into a cup of coffee and she had no fire to light another. perhaps she smokes all night, or perhaps there is an undying cigarette which burns eternally in her bedroom'

—iris murdoch, *under the net*

i don't know how things got to be this way, but i hope you'll take the parts of me that you love and want—books, clothes and otherwise. and when summer comes around, listen to the cure in a car speeding to wildwood, nj and think of me.

know that I love you all.
trisha.

Article III
Executor and Administrative Powers

dear josef,

if you're reading this, i guess i'm gone. i guess i just didn't feel like i could tell you much, so i just in case, this is how i've been feeing. at about three o'clock this afternoon, the volume got turned way down, and i began to realise, i don't do things by halves and yet, i have rather a limited knowledge of you as a person. perhaps i should have known this long before, but it is evident that you don't quite want for our physical relations to continue, or at the very least you are unsure. i am no better—i purport to know what i want, but of course, people are fluid, minds change. i only know that it is probably wise that we continue getting to know each other as just friends, or friends-of-friends, whichever works.

[…]

this is not a love letter, nor is it a letter of longing, although it is couched in similar vocabulary. this is a letter between equals. (kind of maybe).

i think it has become clear that sometimes sleeping with a friend means it easy to imagine that the feel of clothing coming off is the same as encountering real flesh, and that the rawness of kissing is the same as approaching another's heart. it is not.

[…]

I is haunted. I is always, before knowing anything, an I-love-you.
—Derrida on Cixous.

the past always comes back, and I think for all parties involved, it is dangerous. i fancy myself impul-sive, and i start at the extreme, but perhaps you prefer starting at the beginning, and for you, i began at the very end.

[…]

some synonyms for the term 'loose woman': adulteress, fornicatress, hussy, strumpet, trollop, jade, slut, romantic.

[…]

traditionally pejorative terms are easy for me incorporate into my perception of self, but they are never useful for the way i'd like to be in reality. when I first saw you, I wanted to bed you because, well, you're cute, and I thought you had this devil-may-care air about you. something in your face that suggested you knew what you liked, and you'd know what you wanted. easy, I thought, when people know what they want. if he's agreeable, we'll fuck and I'll leave, and perhaps we can get to know each other as friends after. hey, a girl's got needs, after all. but i overestimated myself, and perhaps you, also.

i said to you once, I'm not afraid to fall in love for twenty minutes—i'm not. I just forget that most of the time, loving has consequences, and sometimes, it lingers.

[...]

a dialogue:

1: do you like him?
2: no, i just want to know if we're going to sleep together again, because i don't want to be pre-sumptuous, get my hopes up. you know.
1: you like him.
2: i want to fuck him.
1: it's the same.
2: i don't even know him.

[...]

just fucking is a parody of caring. there are affections that come with it, but they skate on the surface, performative actions that signify physical connections but lack any kind of internality. there is always room in the margins of the present for desire, but it is fleeting, and once satisfied, begins again, a knot at the base of the belly that moves up against your throat. just fucking can kill you.

[...]

a lover wrote this to me once: 'I think I'm entering the final stage of this videogame. You can tell it's the end because it's always night and the enemies are harder. The soundtrack is a compilation of the motifs which graced earlier levels, and the level itself is designed to be an anthology of levels beaten. Sometimes you have to fight all the end-level bosses again, in succession. And there's the ultimate evil waiting at the end. And then probably some badly-written expository message of con-gratulations wedged in right before the end credits: here are the people who had a hand in bring-ing this experience to you, presented as white text on a black background scrolling up and away. If you look closer though, bored by the list of collaborators, you see your own reflection in the glassy screen. You did this to yourself. Play again (Y/N)?'

[…]

if you haven't noticed, this is, as always, an apology. someone once said to me that i apologise when i'm looking for a specific something in return. it's a proffering, a reaching out for someone to engage with this empty language that doesn't quite have a net. (footnote: Barthes) I don't know if it's true, but i certainly believe i might have backed you into a situation you weren't looking for in the first place.

in other words: i thought i wanted just a moment. and then i wanted it again.

[…]

'You are authorized to use the X Services (regardless of whether your access or use is intended) only if you agree to abide by all applicable laws, rules and regulations ('Applicable Law') and the terms of this Agreement. In addition, in consideration for becoming a Member and/or making use of the X Services, you must indicate your acceptance of this Agreement during the registration process.'

i have violated the terms of this agreement.

[…]

i like speaking in cliches because the funny thing is, more often than not, they're true.

trisha.

Article IV
Guardianship Provisions

dear trisha,

this morning i had a dream that you had turned your bedroom into a replica of kindergarten & taken to running through it dressed the part, smashing over towers of blocks, hiding in a bathtub full of stuffed animals, doing things like learning to spell, just for a lark, doing something that was like 'finding the origin' of some particular thread of creative thought you'd been following back along the ground of your life for a long time. but i can't be more specific, because all of this information arrived to me—that is, presented itself to the eye of the dream's camera—in the form of an old, beat-up video tape that had been found unlabeled in a stack at a garage sale. this was a video about you & your poetics as though you were a great artist of the 1970s & the version of you that currently exists is a reincarnation of her, a second time around, because your work was not yet done before whatever happened happened. the video featured the you of today dressed as this kindergartener with big tigger the tiger slippers narrating in between sucking on a lollipop over footage of the 1970s you, talking about how you thought that the 1970s you was 'such a cunt' & that you couldn't possibly be her, you didn't 'see the resemblance,' that this was all a fiction devised by your literary agent— agent willis, a man that was like a straightened out hook you'd pull out of your finger, but shinier in the hair—& you just wanted to *get back to playing with your toys*. then you rolled your eyes, snorted, tossed your hair back, & video you did a vertical scan error thing that made the TV fall end over end backwards off the table & a ghostly puff came out of the wreck that made everyone at the garage sale purchase whatever they were holding immediately & then they headed home, feverish to scribble down the thoughts that had just occurred to them. at this point i appeared in the dream. i was at my desk in my current room & about to read a book by the you of the 1970s, & then i woke up.

love,
thomson.

addenda: sometimes you were wearing this dark plaid dress & shiny black buckle shoes, sometimes these big pajamas.

agent willis, as your literary agent, was in charge of discovering your reincarnations, like they have those people that find the dalai lama.

General Provisions

If any beneficiary or beneficiaries of this Will shall contest the Will or in any manner attempt to have it or any trust or beneficial interest created by it declared invalid, such person or persons shall receive no benefits from or interests under this Will and my Will shall be carried out as if such person or persons had pre-deceased me.

I have entered neither into a contract to make wills nor into a contract not to revoke wills. Any similarity of the provisions of my Will to the provisions of the will of my witnesses or any other person, if any, executed on the same or on different dates than my Will, shall not be construed of as evidence of such a contract.

Unless specifically set forth in writing and acknowledged by the donee thereof, of any gift I have made or will make during my lifetime shall not be treated as satisfaction, in whole or in part, of any device or bequest in my Will.

On this 1st July, 2011 in the City of New York, State of New York, I hereby sign this document and declare it to be my last will.

In Memory of Trisha Low
(1988-2012)

Last Will & Testament of Trisha Low

I, Trisha Low of the City of New York, State of New York, USA, declare that this is my Last Will & Testament.

Article I
Preliminary Declarations

It's enough to die of spite.

xoxo,
trisha.

General Provisions

If any beneficiary or beneficiaries of this Will shall contest the Will or in any manner attempt to have it or any trust or beneficial interest created by it declared invalid, such person or persons shall receive no benefits from or interests under this Will and my Will shall be carried out as if such person or persons had pre-deceased me.

I have entered neither into a contract to make wills nor into a contract not to revoke wills. Any similarity of the provisions of my Will to the provisions of the will of my witnesses or any other person, if any, executed on the same or on different dates than my Will, shall not be construed of as evidence of such a contract.

Unless specifically set forth in writing and acknowledged by the donee thereof, of any gift I have made or will make during my lifetime shall not be treated as satisfaction, in whole or in part, of any device or bequest in my Will.

On this August 16th, 2012 in the City of New York, State of New York, I hereby sign this document and declare it to be my last will.

VOL. II: THE SEXUAL ASSAULT OF TRISHA LOW
AS CIRCULATED BY LOVE IN A MAZE,
OR, VIRTUE REWARDED.

for Andy Martrich, who killed me.

'The subject says to the object: "I destroyed you," and the object is there to receive the communication. From now on the subject says: "Hullo, object!" "I destroyed you." "I love you." "You have value for me because of your survival of my destruction of you." "While I am loving you I am all the time destroying you in (unconscious) fantasy." Here fantasy begins for the individual.'

–D. W. Winnicott, *Playing and Reality.*

'Sometimes we must willfully and wrongly create our fathers before we try to kill them.'

– Aliza Shvarts.

SIR or DOCTOR;

I sit down to give you an undeniable proof of my considering your desires as indispensable orders. Ungracious then as the task may be, I shall recall to view those scandalous stages of my life out of which I emerg'd at length to the enjoyment of every blessing in the power of love, health and fortune to bestow; whilst yet in the flower of youth and not too late to employ the leisure afforded me by great ease and affluence. To cultivate an understanding—naturally not a despicable one, and which had, even amidst the whirl of loose pleasures I had been tost in, exerted more observation on the characters and manners of the world, than what is common to those of my unhappy womanly profession—who looking on all thought or reflexion as their capital enemy, keep it at as great a distance as they can, or destroy it without mercy. We must speak plainly. We must avoid all self-deception. We must shirk no particulars.

Hating as I mortally do, all long unnecessary prefaces, I shall give you good quarter in this, and use no farther apology than to prepare you for seeing the loose part of my life, wrote with the same liberty that I led it. It is a case of oil and water.

Truth! Stark naked truth, is the word, and I will assure you I will not so much as take the pains to bestow the strip of a Band-Aid on it, to paint situations such as they *actually* rose to me in nature, careless of violating those laws of decency, that were never made for such unreserved intimacies as ours; and you have too much sense, too much knowledge of the *originals* themselves to snuff prudishly and out of character, at the *pictures* of them.

When taxed with it I shall not deny them stoutly. These are scenes in the street. Fierce accusations and disgraceful retorts. One should not give any one any reason to say that little girls are Wicket Little Fibs. My mother would not believe it of me and he could scarcely believe it of himself.

SIR or DOCTOR,
Yours,
ANTHONY ROSSOMANDO as TRISHA LOW &c. &c. &c.

SIR or DOCTOR;

I hope your heart BLEEDS for your DISTRESS and the TEMPTATIONS I am tried with. As so ordered, you will find here The Confession of How Girlish Fits Can Really Be Cured—One BAPTISM might continue to be DEFERRED but dear ANTHONY ROSSOMANDO as TRISHA LOW Will Not Be Cheated Out of Happiness!

AND SO, she broke bread.

fabrizio moretti – The Strokes: December 13 2004, 19:32:57 UTC

[[hey girl, he's yours now, you can do what you with him]]
[[also my boyfriend hates my lipliner! What the fuck! I'm like, leave this apartment!]]

sighs
opens mouth to say something
figures now is not the best time to have a serious conversation
will bring it up later, though
kisses back slowly
slows down even more, squeezing tighter
sucks at your Adam's apple

Please what?

groans as you scratch down spine
breathing into your ear

So fucking hot..

keeps jerking you off teasingly slowly
pulls back a little, just enough to suck own fingers into mouth, eyes on you

anthony rossomando – The Dirty Pretty Things: December 13 2004, 23:10:50 UTC

[[does he really not mind that you're on here?]]

(whimpers, putting arms round your neck and pulling you close)
(whispers against your lips)

Please fuckin' get me off already—

(eyes roll back as you suck at Adam's apple)
(hips jerk up uncontrollably)
(reaches down to feel if you're hard again)
(smirks, grinds own hips against yours
(whispers in your ear, licks)

Do I turn you on? D'you wanna fuck me?

(watches you through eyelashes)

fabrizio moretti – The Strokes: December 13 2004, 23:20:05 UTC

[[oh he thinks it's funny plus it means I'm less like, aggro and pms-ey most of the time.]]

smirks

Not yet. Gonna have to be patient.

kisses right under your ear

I promise you won't regret it.

buries face in your neck as you reach down
rolls hips
groans

I *always* want to fuck you.

drools all over fingers
licks lips
kisses deeply
pushes a finger into you, moving it in an out for a moment before adding a second one

anthony rossomando – The Dirty Pretty Things: December 13 2004, 23:29:11 UTC

[[hahahah, really?]]

(whines in back of throat)

I should have know, you fucking *tease*

(shivers as you kiss ear)

112

(mouths your jaw, pants against the skin open-mouthed)
(reaches down to grab your ass, pulls you closer as you roll hips)

Well, I'm always up for a fuck, so—

(moans against your neck as you lick fingers)
(kisses eagerly, sucking at your lower lip)
(sighs as you push fingers into me)
(leans back, watches your face, twirls fingers in your hair)

fabrizio moretti – The Strokes: December 13 2004, 23:50:54 UTC

[[no more panic attacks! ☺plus]]

breathless laugh

You love it.

whimpers loudly

That really works out well, then.

takes fingers out
wraps them around self
moves between your legs, barely pushing tip into you

Fucking love to fuck you, Stan.. Love the way you feel.

kisses hard
jerks you off harder
pushes in impossibly slowly
groans
rolls hips

anthony rossomando – The Dirty Pretty Things: December 13 2004, 23:59:17 UTC

[[awwww. Delly! Yeah, jane told me what happened.]]

(twines fingers with your other hand, by my head)
(licks lips, watches you)
(whines as you start pushing in)
(tries to press back against you)
(groans in frustration)

God, fuck me please

(tongues your teeth as we kiss)
(hips buck forward)
(grazes your lips with own again)

So fucking hot—

(leans to bite your neck hard, then sucks gently)

fabrizio moretti – The Strokes: December 14 2004, 00:34:36 UTC

[[yeah my boy's great. he even knew me before the whole subway thing happened. and like, after that it really used to all disgust me. like i couldn't think about sex–related subjects without wanting to puke, not even in movies or anything so having Fab, and doing this kind of sorted that out kind of KIND OF]]

squeezes your hand
shakes head

Be patient. Or I'll tease you even more.

leans forward, resting forehead against yours

But maybe that's what you want?

sucks your tongue in
pulls back
pushes back in just as slowly
moans when you bite neck
squeezes you hard
grins
lets go of you
brings your hand down
whispers against your lips

Wanna watch you jerk yourself off.

anthony rossomando – The Dirty Pretty Things: December 14 2004, 15:16:57 UTC

[[yeah. I'm sorry dude. that sounds awful. men suck. not your boy though, like really–at least you felt like you could]]

(gasps against your lips as you rest forehead)
(swears under breath)

(grits teeth, tries not to press forward)

I love a slow tease, but fuck, this is just cruel

(licks slowly around the bite, letting eyelashes flutter against your skin)
(whimpers as you squeeze, then let go)
(smiles against your lips)

(runs hands down your back)

Tell me what you want to see.

(bites your ear gently)

Am I allowed to make myself come

(sucks on the lobe, strokes self once, moaning loudly)

Or do you wanna see me try to excercise my self-control?

fabrizio moretti – The Strokes: December 14 2004, 17:45:23 UTC

[[it's ok. You get jumped on a subway platform is getting jumped on a subway platform. Got to make peace, plus he's been really patient and stuck around It's good to have people? thank god for the internet. That and lip liner is all I have to live for]]

smiles
rolls hips slowly

I'm not cruel..

stops moving
breathes against your lips

This is cruel.

watches you for a second, then starts moving again
tilts head when you lick
shivers as you run your hands down
hips jerk a little when you bite earlobe
looks down to see you touch yourself
lets out a low groan
looks up at your face again

Want to see you come.

deep slow kiss, hips moving a little faster
pulls out before slamming back in hard

Come for me, Stan.

anthony rossomando – The Dirty Pretty Things: December 14 2004, 18:15:10 UTC

[[but he doesn't like your lipliner! Strike one! Fuck everything.]]

(tilts head back)
(moans needily)
(cries out in frustration when you stop)
(tangles both hands in your hair and drags you forward, kisses bruisingly)
(licks at your cheekbone, bites your earlobe again, harder)
(strokes self languidly, then speeds up)
(bites lip, looks up at you almost pleadingly)
(whimpers, runs thumb over the tip of own cock)
(kisses back, bumping noses with you)
(whispers, panting)

Fuck, I'm gonna– Oh, Christ

(cries out as you slam in)
(arches back and comes hard)

fabrizio moretti – The Strokes: December 14 2004, 18:26:31 UTC

[[I know, it's his one failing. But I'll strike it from the strikes. I'll also strike that I'm never lonely because I'm never alone unless I'm here? Like I start to feel lonely, but he won't let me cause he's so paranoid post-incident. There's no such thing as being alone when he's with me all the time so this is kind of crucial time I have here...]]

licks lips when you cry out
might be enjoying torturing you like this a little too much
kisses back
bites your bottom lip
tugs on it
curses under breath when you bite earlobe again
shifts, changing angle of thrusts
moves faster, slamming into you hard

drops head to your shoulder
bites down hard
grips one of your hips tight
looks up when you whisper
moans

So fucking beautiful..

tenses all over
slams in one last time
comes hard, hips jerking uncontrollably

anthony rossomando – The Dirty Pretty Things: December 14 2004, 18:38:40 UTC

[[hahahahaha I guess no one's perfect]]

(closes eyes, gasping)
(tries to get breath back)
(is quite spineless)
(still a little breathless)

Fuck, don't get complacent or anything, but you're fucking good in bed.

(lifts hand to mouth)
(starts licking at it absently)
(strokes your cheek)
(smiles at you)

fabrizio moretti – The Strokes: December 14 2004, 18:44:21 UTC

[[yeah, he gets pretty close.]]
[[dude this thread ruled, they are so good together! Our boys!]]

tries not to collapse on you completely
takes a few moments to get breath back a little
chuckles
kisses softly

You're not bad either.

pulls out, moaning
settles next to you

puts hand on your hip, stroking it
licks lips when you start licking your hand
leans into your hand
smiles back
leans in and kisses again

anthony rossomando – The Dirty Pretty Things: December 14 2004, 18:55:15 UTC

[[why thank you, madam. And nice doing business with you too.]]

(kisses back, lingering)
(smiles shyly)

Why, thank you.

(whimpers, bites lip a little as you pull out)
(pulls you closer as you settle close)
(ghosts fingers up your side)
(makes face at other hand am licking)
(kisses back sweetly)

fabrizio moretti – The Strokes: December 14 2004, 19:03:46 UTC

[[yay! Let's wrap it up though, I gotta go out and have dinner with some friends and probably many martinis]]

laughs

You're welcome.

pushes hair away from your face
traces cheekbone with thumb
smiles when you make a face
moves as close as possible
rests forehead against yours
bites lip

Not gonna leave you, okay?

searches your eyes

I know I've been less than perfect. I disappeared on you, left a note that I was going away with Nick, of all people.. But I'm not going anywhere, I promise.

laughs

You're welcome.

Not gonna leave you, okay?

I know I've been less than perfect. I disappeared on you, left a note that I was going away with Nick, of all people.. But I'm not going anywhere, I promise.

In the bosom of Love in a Maze, TRISHA LOW gathr'd only uncorrupt sweets of VIRTUE, where looking back on the course of VICE she had run and comparing its infamous blandishments with the infinitely superior joys of innocence, she could not help pitying even in point of taste, those who, immers'd in a gross sensuality, are insensible to the so delicate charms of VIRTUE, than which even PLEASURE has not a greater friend, nor than VICE a greater enemy. The sinister ANTHONY ROS-SOMANDO had no opportunity—he was duly upbraided for the concealment of his falsehood, and in the matter of his being seized, convinced all that he could not be innocent of favouring PASSION.
His vizard slipping to one side as he took his AUDIENCE into his arms, they soon discovered enough of that OTHER face they adored less, knowing that it was themselves that had took this method to gain him in the first place. 'I will not,' he wept, 'trouble you with any recital of what I endured from the knowledge of my self-induced misfortune, but you may judge it all only by my LOVE. You were the LOVE of my life. However, I, up against this oppressive weight, have resolved to struggle with my FATE even for the last. I have at least had my worst FEARS confirmed by your behaviours, the FEARS I had believed before, that you, the AUDIENCE, were all along assistants in my DESIGN.' Later he was found gagged to death, legs falling to one side his eyes bulging out of his head, his last words echoing 'No, no, I'm not comfortable with this,' the AUDIENCE chanting 'Come on, just a little bit? You owe us. You owe us this.'

SIR or DOCTOR;

I must needs say, that your Letter has fill'ed me with much TROUBLE. For it has made my HEART, which was overflowing with GRATITUDE, suspicious and fearful. As so ordered, you will find here The Case of How The Old Superstition Became Only Too True—Honesty Isn't <u>Always</u> The Best Policy. Just think of that.

~*~

[[ugh no, the photocopier? i hate it. so not worth my time do you name inanimate objects, you weirdo?]]

grins

Nah, it's just that sometimes you talk like you're old and wise..

You're really not, you know.

smiles

takes your wrist as you walk past
tugs you closer
kisses quickly
eyes light up

We should make French toast.

anthony rossomando – The Dirty Pretty Things: January 11 2005, 20:06:52 UTC

[[yeah, close to everything. my bass guitar's called miffy and my laptop's name is rei]]

(strokes chin and raises eyebrow)

I *am* wise. And I'm older than you anyway.

(moves closer to you)

(bumps nose against yours after we kiss)

Hey, yeah, sounds good. Do we have maple syrup?

fabrizio moretti – The Strokes: January 11 2005, 20:11:13 UTC

[[Cute! do you guys have a gig coming up soon? Also I won't lie to you… The Menacing Archivists is a pretty terrifying band name.]]

snorts

Yeah, sure you are.

grins

I keep forgetting you're actually a craddle robber.
looks up at you
makes a face

Maple syrup on French toast? What's wrong with you?

anthony rossomando – The Dirty Pretty Things: January 11 2005, 20:21:27 UTC

[[yeah dude. at harrow, the only all girl band. they have so much equipment there, a recording studio and everything! jealous.]]
[[also, if by terrifying, you mean shit. yes. unfortunately we're stuck with it.]]

(puts arms around your waist)

I'm not. I just like you. And don't flatter yourself, you're not that young.

(looks surprised)

Dude, everything tastes good with maple syrup on. Especially French toast.

(takes your hand and drags you into kitchen)

Come on, don't be sulky.

fabrizio moretti – The Strokes: January 11 2005, 20:25:07 UTC

[[is the idea that things work better if they're named, because definitely do not want to unclog the fucking photocopier 100 times tomorrow]]

laughs

Hey, in case you didn't know, calling me old isn't gonna help you get in my pants today.

rolls eyes, amused

I never said maple syrup was bad.

But it's not how you make French toast.

pouts

I'm not sulky!

follows you and goes to fridge
gets eggs and milk out

anthony rossomando – The Dirty Pretty Things: January 11 2005, 20:28:45 UTC

[[yeah, always worked for me, even when I spilled hot chocolate all over my laptop. Twice.]]

(looks over shoulder)

Who said I wanted in your pants today? Don't be presumptuous.

(rolls eyes, laughing)

Fine, fine, you make it, then.

(swipes finger over your bottom lip)

Look at that mouth. Honestly.

(sits on kitchen counter, watching you.)

fabrizio moretti – The Strokes: January 11 2005, 20:35:40 UTC

[[speaking of cute, though, look at these two, so domestic.]]
[[also sugar will totally eat your laptop inside out–be careful! I don't know what Fab and I would do without you!]]

chuckles
wraps arms around you from behind
kisses between your shoulderblades
whispers

You always want in my pants.

lets go
grins

Alright. French toast, coming up.

bites your finger

glances at you

I thought you were gonna make some coffee?

sets eggs and milk down
grabs bread and sugar

anthony rossomando – The Dirty Pretty Things: January 11 2005, 20:53:46 UTC

[[oh i know, I love them together. And nick, so jealous, so violent, so doesn't have a chance.]]

(leans a little back into you)

Well. I'm convincable. But not always.

(taps your nose)
(hops off counter)

God, yeah, I can't believe I forgot.

(sets to making coffee)

So…how's life.

(looks over)

Hey, I didn't know you needed milk for french toast.

fabrizio moretti – The Strokes: January 11 2005, 20:58:50 UTC

[[well he might be married, but Fab's easily tempted and you know what Kat's like with him, the two of them together are dynamite-esque unpredictable.]]

smirks

Sure you can say no.

laughs

Airhead.

starts making French toast
hums quietly
frowns a little and shrugs

Life's alright.

Why do you ask? I mean, you were there. You know what's going on.

looks up
grins

Looks like you've got a lot to learn.

anthony rossomando – The Dirty Pretty Things: January 11 2005, 21:02:36 UTC

[[Uh oh something's brewing. She's staying with a friend, right?]]

(grins)

You don't believe me?

(chuckles)

Am not! I just have, you know. A tendency to forget things.

(listens)

Bet you can sing. You just won't to spite me.

(shrugs)

Just felt like I should say something.

(raises eybrows)

Oh, you've taught me plenty already.

(watches as coffee machine starts filtering coffee)

fabrizio moretti – The Strokes: January 11 2005, 21:11:44 UTC

[[yep, she's back on. i'm sure she'll be looking for you soon…mwahahahaha]]

grins

Oh, I believe you actually think you could. But you couldn't.

Riiight. And that doesn't make you a complete airhead?

rolls eyes

No, if I wanted to spite you I'd sing when I'm around other people. I don't.

smiles

You know, silence is good sometimes, too.

smirks

Oh yeah, like what?

turns to you

Maybe I should quiz you again.

anthony rossomando – The Dirty Pretty Things: January 11 2005, 21:19:27 UTC

[[ugh, well now, see, you made Stan sad.]]

(smirks)

Well. For me to know and you to find out.

(sulks)

No, just…forgetful.

(smiles)

I know. I'm just messing with you. Anyway.

(starts pouring coffee)
(awkwardly)

I know. It's just, you know. Wow, I'm seriously incoherent today.

(raises eyebrows more)

You *could*, but that would involve me getting in your pants. You wouldn't want that, would you?

fabrizio moretti – The Strokes: January 11 2005, 21:24:00 UTC

[[☹☹☹ I'm sorry baby but it's a complicated world.]]

laughs

I intend to.

teasingly

Who's being sulky, now?

I know you're joking. Don't worry.

puts French toast on plates
sets them on table
sits down
looks up at you

Something bugging you?

grins

I never said that.

anthony rossomando – The Dirty Pretty Things: January 11 2005, 21:30:54 UTC

[[oh NOOOOOOO!]]

(chuckles)

All right, then.

(pouts)

Well, both of us can be sulky, right. And I think in my case, it was more justified anyway.

(passes you a fresh cup of coffee)

There you go.

(sits down too)
(half smiles)

No, not really.

(laughs)

I've backed myself in a corner now.

fabrizio moretti – The Strokes: January 11 2005, 21:35:54 UTC

[[welcome to our teacup world of fantasy-level-drama]]

grins

Don't worry, you're gonna love it.

chuckles

You can be fuckin' adorable, you know that?

takes coffee

sips

Mmm, fuckin' excellent.

takes a bite of French toast
watches you intently
decides to drop it this time
nods

Can only blame yourself. I'm completely innocent.

anthony rossomando – The Dirty Pretty Things: January 11 2005, 21:41:03 UTC

[[my life is finally fantasy-level-drama already! I don't need this delly!]]

(watches you intently)

If you say so.

(laughs, going red)

I'm not *adorable*. That's like, what you'd call a dalmation, not me.

(gulps down coffee)

God, I wanted some caffeine.

(munches on french toast)

(eyes widen)

Mm. This is nicer than normal French toast.

(nods agreeably)

My bad, sorry.

fabrizio moretti – The Strokes: January 11 2005, 21:45:40 UTC

[[mwahahahahahaha, wait what's wrong?]]

smirks

Trust me, man.

smiles

Fine. Not adorable.

But still really fuckin' cute.

licks lips

Fuck, me too. You make some really good coffee, you know. I might just keep you around.

smugly

I know. I'm good.

grins

It's alright, I think I'll find it in my heart to forgive you.

anthony rossomando – The Dirty Pretty Things: January 11 2005, 21:50:00 UTC

[[oh, just edd. the usual. he called me to hang out and i don't know if he means 'hang out' because he's seeing this new girl because i don't know if he's going to cheat on her with me like he did with the last 'new girl,' god my life is a joke]]

(smiles)

I do. Perhaps more than you think, actually.

(throws a piece of french toast at you)

Oi! Same thing. I resent that.

(watchs you sip coffee, winks)

Well, if you put me out, I'd be on the streets, probably turning tricks for money. So I'm glad I you like my coffee.

(eats more toast)

Arrogant bastard.

(looks up, amused)

Thank you, O great and wonderful one.

fabrizio moretti – The Strokes: January 11 2005, 21:54:22 UTC

[[sounds like a real stable, secure, healthy thing you got going on there]]

smiles and says nothing
catches piece of toast and pops it into mouth

What do you want me to say, then?

grins

I keep you around for more than just your coffee, man.

laughs

You fucking love it.

makes face

That makes me sound like an ass.

Just call me Master.

anthony rossomando – The Dirty Pretty Things: January 11 2005, 22:00:01 UTC

[[UGH shut up]]

(laughs as you eat toast)

Well.

(considers)

Well, I know you like me, and that's more than enough. And perhaps on a good day, I won't have an objection to being described as a teddy bear would.

(raises eyebrow)

Oh yeah? You keep me here for my stimulating conversation, of course.

(chokes on coffee)

Yeah, you do sound like an ass.

(studies you for a moment, shrugs almost imperceptibly)

Makes it sound like you want to punish me... Master.

fabrizio moretti – The Strokes: January 11 2005, 22:05:31 UTC

[[babe, you're 16. it's what you're supposed to be doing]]

sips coffee as you speak
grins

You'd make a great teddy bear. You're cuddly enough. I might have to get you a big red bow.

seriously

Obviously. I love the way we can spend hours.. *discussing important matters.*

laughs

Thanks for your support, man.

smirks

Maybe I do.

sits back

amused

Keep talking, I like the sound of it.

teasingly

I'd never be able to fuck you again after that.

anthony rossomando – The Dirty Pretty Things: January 11 2005, 22:09:55 UTC

[[yeah, like it's totally my fault and my job to be a hot mess right now.]]

(chokes again)

Please God, no. I'm not *actually* a teddy bear. You do know this, right? I have no objection to being likened to a teddy bear but…

(equally seriously)

Oh yeah. Very important matters.

(leans over, ruffles your hair)

Anytime.

(blushes)

Nah. It was just a thought.

fabrizio moretti – The Strokes: January 11 2005, 22:15:12 UTC

[[that and kicking ass at school]]

laughs

Fine, you're not a teddy bear.

Some other kind of stuffed animal, then. A poodle?

slow smile

You're nice to talk to, you know? You can put forward some pretty good ideas.

grabs your wrist

grins

Well then, elaborate. I think there's a lot of potential there.

anthony rossomando – The Dirty Pretty Things: January 11 2005, 22:18:18 UTC

[[and I do! Suck it English essay, you can take that A+ and Mr Forbes said my portfolio was outstanding.]]

(chokes for a third time)

God, you're trying to kill me, aren't you? No comment.

(looks awkward)

Uhuh. Some. Not all the time, though.

(tries to pull away)
(blushes more)
(then looks up, almost shyly)

Well, if you wanted to punish me…you want me on my knees, Master?

fabrizio moretti – The Strokes: January 11 2005, 22:25:05 UTC

grins
shakes head

Nah, contrary to what you seem to think, I like having you alive.

smiles

No, I'm serious. Of course, it helps that we end up.. agreeing.

strokes inside of your wrist with thumb
shakes head

Don't want to punish you. No need to when you're being so good, anyway.

looks at you
sighs
lets go of you
gathers dirty dishes

walks to sink and starts washing them

anthony rossomando – The Dirty Pretty Things: January 11 2005, 22:28:36 UTC

[[owtch, girl, rejection much?]]

(smiles)

Well, I quite like being alive.

(chuckles)

That's probably the best bit.

(looks at you, confused)
(swallows a little)
(clears throat)
(blushes really red)

Uh, I guess. Sorry?

(sits on a kitchen chair, with knees to chest, looking out the window)

fabrizio moretti – The Strokes: January 11 2005, 22:34:53 UTC

[[mm. i don't know dude. this was just going like, not my way.]]

laughs

Then it all works out perfectly.

grins

I like agreeing with you, yeah. But the whole conversation leading to it is also quite fulfilling. Intellectually, of course.

keeps back to you
bites lip when you apologize
finishes washing dishes
dries hands and turns back to you

What are you sorry for? You didn't do anything wrong, Stan.

anthony rossomando – The Dirty Pretty Things: January 11 2005, 22:38:21 UTC

[[can we not talk about this right now?]]

(winks)

I'd have to agree there.

(runs hand through hair)
(puts chin on knees)
(looks down, bites lip)

I don't know. Usually it fixes things.

(shrugs)

You looked like I upset you.

fabrizio moretti – The Strokes: January 11 2005, 22:49:07 UTC

takes a deep breath
walks up to you
grabs chair and sits right in front of you
brings hand to your chin
tilts your head up

You didn't upset me, and there's nothing to fix.

leans in and kisses gently

I'm just not the kind of guy who gets off on being called 'Master'

anthony rossomando – The Dirty Pretty Things: January 11 2005, 22:57:55 UTC

(can't meet your eyes)

Good.

(gulps a little)
(kisses back chastely)
(pulls back)
(sighs shakily)

You know what the funny thing is? I don't like that shit either. I guess… I don't know.

fabrizio moretti – The Strokes: January 11 2005, 23:03:44 UTC

sighs

Will you just fucking look at me?

rests forehead against yours
strokes your jaw
softly

You've got to stop doing stuff just because you think it's what I want.

It's not how it works, Stan.

shakes head imperceptibly
pulls back
looks at you for a moment
gets up and goes to counter
leans against it and lights a cigarette

I don't know what the fuck happened to you that you'd think so.

Things aren't supposed to be easy, and that's part of what makes it interesting.

anthony rossomando – The Dirty Pretty Things: January 12 2005, 11:52:52 UT

(looks away again)
(pulls sleeves down over hands)
(quietly)

I know. You're right. It's stupid of me to try and make things easier for myself because it'll never happen. But something's gotta give, you know? I hate antagonism, and if it can be prevented, then why the fuck not?

fabrizio moretti – The Strokes: January 12 2005, 12:43:02 UTC

smokes quietly, watching you
small smile
crushes cigarette and walks back to you
pulls you up

It's not stupid to try and make things easier.

But it's stupid to think doing everything the other wants is going to achieve that.

If anything, it'll make it harder in the end.

kisses

Let's make a deal.

You're going to stop acting like you think I want you to act.

And I'm going to stop pretending everything's always fine.

anthony rossomando – The Dirty Pretty Things: January 12 2005, 13:20:34 UTC

(looks up as you walk over)
(stands up, tripping a little)
(sighs, pushes your hair back)
(closes eyes as you kiss)
(chuckles softly)

Sounds fair. Well, I'll try anyway.

(kisses again)
(pauses a moment)

Okay, so do you mind me asking…

This thing with Nick. Is it always going to come above you and me? Or is there even really a you and me?

(watches you carefully, hopes you don't get angry)

fabrizio moretti – The Strokes: January 12 2005, 18:04:52 UTC

[[sorry, I didn't mean to snap]]

sets hands on your hips, stroking softly
grins

It's good enough for me.

kisses back

opens mouth
sucks on your bottom lip
looks disappointed when you pull back
sighs
takes a minute to think about best way to explain

I don't know. I mean.. I don't know what's gonna happen with..this thing. He's my best friend, I'm always going to love him. I can't imagine not loving him.

pulls you closer

But I like you. I *really* like you. And as far as I'm concerned, there's a you and me. There'll be one as long as you'll have me, man

laughs nervously

Fuck, you realize you're turning me into a fucking girl here?

anthony rossomando – The Dirty Pretty Things: January 12 2005, 19:41:31 UTC

(listens to you)

I know you're always going to love him, Fab, but there's a difference between loving him and being *in* love with him.

(puts arms around your waist)

Okay. I can cope with that. For the moment anyway.

(brushes your hair back)

You have girly hair anyway. It suits you.

fabrizio moretti – The Strokes: January 12 2005, 22:17:58 UTC

[[trisha? Are you okay?]]

holds you tighter

I can't tell you I'm gonna stop being in love with him or anything. Because I don't know that.

relieved
nods

'For the moment' is a good start, right?

smiles
sticks tongue out at you
runs one hand through your hair

You're one to talk..

anthony rossomando – The Dirty Pretty Things: January 15 2005, 17:32:49 UTC

[[sorry, my internet was brokes, and then school started checking up on me... they tracked my online activity for a couple of days]]

(leans into you)

I know. It was an unfair question anyway, I'm sorry.

(kisses you softly)

Yeah. It'll do.

(nips at your tongue)

Yours is longer...

fabrizio moretti – The Strokes: January 15 2005, 17:38:13 UTC

[[Aw, stupid Internet!! I missed you! What are you on probation for?]]

shakes head
almost inaudible

s'okay.

kisses back
smiles

I swear you won't regret it.

laughs
shoves playfully

What, you want me to cut it off?

anthony rossomando – The Dirty Pretty Things: January 15 2005, 17:55:17 UTC

[[the usual. knives, skipping rope, trying to sell this bitch classmate as a white sex slave on ebay.]]

(keeps stroking your hair)

I hope not.

(laughs as you shove, puts up hands in mock defeat)

Okay, okay, don't! You know I like it

fabrizio moretti – The Strokes: January 15 2005, 18:00:04 UTC

[[HAHAHAHAHA did you get any bids? are you feeling okay? Is Stan feeling okay? Let's start a new thread! Fab's got something to say, and that deserves a new post!]]

grins

Like I would, anyway.

kisses again
watches you
pulls away suddenly

I.. I gotta go. Promised Jules I'd meet up with him today. I'll see you later.

leaves quickly

[[See you in the new post in.. a couple of minutes.. finishing typing! :D]]

fabrizio moretti – The Strokes: January 15 2005, 18:03:32 UTC

[[Posted, and dinner. Back soon, sweets!]]

~*~

In the bosom of Love in a Maze, TRISHA LOW gathr'd only uncorrupt sweets of VIRTUE, where looking back on the course of VICE she had run, and comparing its infamous blandishments with the infinitely superior joys of innocence, she could not help pitying even in point of taste those who, immers'd in a gross sensuality, are insensible to the so delicate charms of VIRTUE, than which even PLEASURE has not a greater friend, nor than VICE a greater enemy. The sinister ANTHONY ROSSOMANDO looked upon himself as the most guilty person upon earth, being the primary cause of all the misfortunes that he had brought upon himself. Not being able to talk, knowing it was without a doubt, his fault for exposing himself thusly, and in such attire, he retired immediately to a monastery; he was now resolved to punish from all he did, or could love, the guilt of indulging that PASSION while it was a CRIME. But unable to live, he attacked his genitals with his assigned tools of meditation crying 'It's a bad omen! It's our Master's way of showing his anger about the spread of sin in the world!' After this unsolicited display of mutilation, his startled AUDIENCE rushed over and demanded that he pull up his trousers unconditionally.

SIR or DOCTOR;

I have a GREAT TROUBLE and SOME COMFORT to acquaint you with. You will find here The Confession of ANTHONY ROSSOMANDO as TRISHA LOW whose Speaking Soon Became Words Which Barred the Door Against Love. Of course, it was nothing but a matter of her BIRTH and EARLY UPBRINGING, Darling Bud.

~*~

fabrizio moretti – The Strokes: January 15 2005 18:00:00

[[babe, we need to talk about this, clearly you're not okay.]]

I honestly didn't think my life could become more complicated.

Of course, I can only blame myself.

—Fab.

anthony rossomando – The Dirty Pretty Things: January 15 2005, 18:05:21 UTC

[[i'm fine. i just had a bad day with school and the boy yesterday.]]

(frowns)
(comes and sits next to you)

Hey, you okay? You look all mopey.

fabrizio moretti – The Strokes: January 15 2005, 18:21:14 UTC

[[he end up blowing you off?]]

looks up at you
smiles drunkenly
shifts so is straddling you on couch
kisses slowly
pulls back, just enough to whisper against your lips

I love you.

anthony rossomando – The Dirty Pretty Things: January 15 2005, 18:30:57 UTC

141

[[yeah. but whatever. he has a new girl, like he always has a new girl, like how I shouldn't have stolen him away from my best friend, it's just karma, i'll be fine]]

(is surprised when you straddle)
(frowns a little)

Fab, are you—

(is cut off by kiss)
(moans softly)
(sighs as you pull back, then eyes widen as you speak)
(bites lips uncertainly)
(strokes your hair back gently)

You don't mean that, love, you're drunk.

fabrizio moretti – The Strokes: January 15 2005, 18:35:48 UTC

[[and school?]]

runs hands down your arms
gently strokes your wrists
looks at you expectantly
leans into your hand
shakes head

No. I mean it.

kisses again

I mean it, Stan.

anthony rossomando – The Dirty Pretty Things: January 15 2005, 18:40:55 UTC

[[i got ratted out about the penknife by dear Georgina and so now they want to take away my scholarship and told my parents. It's just a lot.]]

(shivers as you stroke wrists)
(brings hands down to settle at your waist)
(pulls you closer)
(searches your eyes)
(kisses back deeply, smiles against your lips)

(shakily)

I love you too.

(slides one hand lightly up your back, under your shirt)

fabrizio moretti – The Strokes: January 15 2005, 18:46:40 UTC

[[shit. i'm sorry babe. maybe new nail polish will help? it always does. live for the nail polish, or for Stan, at least. what would fab do without him?]]

sets hands on your shoulders
looks down at you
brings hips flush against yours
lets out a relieved sigh as you kiss back
smiles

I know.

kisses your neck

I'm sorry I'm so fucking stupid and it took me so long.

trails hands down your chest
slides them under your t-shirt

anthony rossomando – The Dirty Pretty Things: January 15 2005, 18:57:45 UTC

[[it's doesn't matter dude. i don't really want to talk about it.]]

(breathes 'oh' as you bring hips together)
(slides tongue along your bottom lip)
(fingers twist in your hair as you kiss neck)

You're not stupid at all—God, I'm just. I'm really glad.

(runs fingers slowly up your spine)
(tugs at hem of your t-shirt with other hand)

fabrizio moretti – The Strokes: January 15 2005, 19:03:42 UTC

[[okay babe, we won't. but maybe we should at least talk about what happened]]

grins
rolls hips slowly
opens mouth and sucks your tongue in
moans when you twist fingers in hair
kisses down your neck to your collarbone
drags fingernails down your stomach
shivers excitedly

So fucking hot..

anthony rossomando – The Dirty Pretty Things: January 16 2005, 14:06:56 UTC

[[o, it's fine.]]

(tilts head)
(sighs blissfully)
(whispers in your mouth)

Fuck, that's good.

(scratches your scalp lightly)
(pushes you back gently to take off your shirt)
(kisses all over your chest)

fabrizio moretti – The Strokes: January 16 2005, 14:13:33 UTC

[[quit it, you're upset]]

grins

Gonna get better, Stan.

undoes button of your jeans
purrs when you scratch
chuckles as is pushed back
lets you take shirt off
kisses slowly
licks lips
slides to floor, kneeling between your legs
looks up at you

anthony rossomando – The Dirty Pretty Things: January 16 2005, 15:34:33 UTC

144

[[i'm always upset, one thing really doesn't make that much of a difference. look delly please just let's stop okay? They're getting along fine, I mean obviously]]

(watches you hotly)
(trails one finger down your cheekbone)

You're so beautiful

(hips buck up slightly as you unbutton)
(kisses back, tonguing your mouth deep)
(watches you as you slide, hand still in your hair)
(leans down, kisses you tenderly on the forehead)

Only if you want to.

fabrizio moretti – The Strokes: January 16 2005, 15:41:26 UTC

[[awwww okay. if you want.]]

turns head
bites your finger gently
toys with elastic of your boxers
moans into kiss
closes eyes, smiling
pulls your zipper down
sets hands on waistband of your jeans
tugs jeans off
leans in again, kissing your stomach
runs fingertips up your thighs

anthony rossomando – The Dirty Pretty Things: January 16 2005, 19:15:03 UTC

[[I'm going to have to go soon cause I'm on restricted internet time, so I don't know if i'm going to be able to finish this thread ☹]]

(watches you, smiling coyly as you bite finger)
(twists a curl around finger)
(moans as you pull zipper down)
(licks lips, watching you)
(closes eyes as you touch)

Mmph. Nice.

fabrizio moretti – The Strokes: January 16 2005, 19:21:46 UTC

[[you in labs or in common room?]]

leans into your touch
grins up at you
runs hands up to your hips
seriously

Not just saying this to get in your pants.

nuzzles happy trail

I love you.

mouthes through underwear

anthony rossomando – The Dirty Pretty Things: January 17 2005, 18:42:40 UTC

[[labs, so a little riskier. plus the internet dudes hate me, they're mean I don't know how like every little squirt of an upper third girl has a crush on them.]]

(rubs at your scalp idly)
(bucks hips again, slightly)
(bites lip as you speak)
(smiles to self)
(shivers as you nuzzle)
(closes eyes)

God, I love you too—Please

fabrizio moretti – The Strokes: January 17 2005, 19:08:13 UTC

[[aw they're young and cute, probably.]]

groans softly
keeps eyes on you
smiles gently
bites at your stomach
tugs your underwear down slowly

What do you want, Stan?

anthony rossomando – The Dirty Pretty Things: January 17 2005, 19:26:04 UTC

[[most of them are balding. One is young and cute.]]

(runs hand through your hair)
(leans down to kiss you demandingly, cupping your face)
(bites at your lips)
(lifts hips to let you bring underwear down)
(whispers against yor lips)

I want you to blow me, then I'm yours to fuck

fabrizio moretti – The Strokes: January 17 2005, 19:38:30 UTC

[[you totally have a crush!!]]

kisses back, parting lips
moans as you bite
licks your lips
grins and wraps fingers around you
strokes slowly

Sounds good to me

leans down and wraps lips around tip

anthony rossomando – The Dirty Pretty Things: January 18 2005, 13:55:06 UTC

[[I don't concern myself with such trivial things]]

(tilts your chin towards me as you stroke)
(gasps, breath quickening)

just love looking at you

(leans down, nuzzles your hair)
(moans into it as you mouth tip)

fabrizio moretti – The Strokes: January 18 2005, 14:07:10 UTC

[[aw sweetie, I really am sorry you're having such a BLAH time. Just know that I'm around, okay?]]

locks eyes with yours
smirks as you breathe faster

You know what I love?

licks up your cock, from base to tip
eyes flicker up to you

I love the way you look at me.

sucks on tip, wetting it
pulls back and blows on it
takes length in
sucks hard, head bobbing up and down

anthony rossomando – The Dirty Pretty Things: January 19 2005, 12:16:45 UTC

[[fuck, delly, i gotta run, i think they're gonna cut me off in a minute. sorry sorry sorry]]

(watches you hotly, mouth open a little)

Uhnh.

(shivers as you lick, clenches thigh muscles a little)
(leans down and kisses you gently)
(groans as you suck on tip)
(tugs on your hair gently)

tease

(cries out as you take length in, grips your hair tighter)

Fuck—Oh, Jesus, fuck—

fabrizio moretti – The Strokes: January 19 2005, 16:42:22 UTC

[[that's okay babe, i'll catch you later, take care of yourself okay?? See you soon?]]

looks smug at your lack of articulate reply
runs fingertips over your inner thighs
then moves hands around to your ass
squeezes it, pulling you closer
moans around you
presses tongue flat against length
whimpers softly as you grip hair tighter

sucks harder
runs fingers over crack of your ass

~*~

In the bosom of Love in a Maze, TRISHA LOW gathr'd only uncorrupt sweets of VIRTUE where looking back on the course of VICE she had run and comparing its infamous blandishments with the infinitely superior joys of innocence, she could not help pitying even in point of taste, those who, immers'd in a gross sensuality, are insensible to the so delicate charms of VIRTUE, than which even PLEASURE has not a greater friend, nor than VICE a greater enemy. The sinister ANTHONY ROSSOMANDO no longer had breath to form denials, or his arm strength to guard or retain the beauteous charge TRISHA LOW. All could see the rage in his eyes and all the strings of disappointment glowing fierce in them. And yet, he had hopes that a general content may crown his bitter end.

'Appear!' he cried, raising his voice. 'Appear! Thou lovely faithful maid, Come forth!'

He had no sooner spoke than he realised he was ever FALSE—for it became apparent that her phantasm would no longer appear. It would haunt him no longer now he was at his lowest. With LOVE and REASON incompatible, INSANITY crept in. Thinking he was unbreakable, he begun scratching himself on an electric pole in a field. He had been informed by the AUDIENCE that doing so would help him sleep but at some point, he realised, he could no longer move his arms or legs. The vibrations had caused overhead wires to touch each other and combust. He remembered the electricity; a thin sliver, half illuminating things and it all seemed like maybe it was still just a dream. He thought it was autumn, or maybe spring. Something pinned him down and he could not focus or keep his eyes open. It just kept going at him, pressing against him. Automatic systems tried in vain to switch over to a standby generator. Sooner or later, the AUDIENCE discovered him fried in a field beneath 11,000-volt cables.

SIR or DOCTOR;

I have been SCARED out of my SENSES. As so ordered, you will find here The Confession of How The Home of Dear and Trusting ANTHONY ROSSOMANDO as TRISHA LOW was to be Dishonoured and Wrecked. 'Seems entertaining to me,' someone said loyally, manifestly sharing the RAPTURE.

~*~

anthony rossomando – The Dirty Pretty Things: March 14 2005 22:02:00

[[he said he just thought I was depressed]]

(chews on pencil grumpily)
(strums a few chords on guitar)
(scribbles things out on a piece of paper)
(is just waiting to be disturbed, really)

–Stan.

fabrizio moretti – The Strokes: March 14 2005, 22:29:33 UTC

[[what?]]

in music room
talking to Fish about the bass line on a song I wrote
hears you
joins you in front room

What?

anthony rossomando – The Dirty Pretty Things: March 14 2005, 22:35:43 UTC

[[edd. i've just been thinking about that thing. that's what he used to say before we broke up. i mean i guess that's why we broke up]]

(starts laughing)
(puts computer down)
(pulls you into my lap)
(hugs you really hard around the middle)
(grinning)

We're gonna be famous and shit!

(pushes you off me)
(but not hard)

Okay, I don't like cuddling.

fabrizio moretti – The Strokes: March 14 2005, 22:37:35 UTC

[[oh yeah? which thing?]]

surprised

What the..

goes with it
ruffles your hair

Aren't we already?

gets off you
sits next to you, though

Why the fuck not?

anthony rossomando –– The Dirty Pretty Things: March 14 2005, 22:39:43 UTC

[[the roofie thing—i mean, I don't think what happened to me is anywhere near as bad as some of the stories on here but it doesn't mean it didn't happen, right?]]

(draws legs up to chest)
(lights another cigarette)

I don't know.

(pats Fab's leg)

I just totally don't.

fabrizio moretti – The Strokes: March 14 2005, 22:42:03 UTC

[[babe, of course not. it's fucked.]]

amused

nods
mock upset

All that stuff they're saying about you is true. You're a cold-hearted bastard, it's terrible.

smiles and looks away

I mean they also all told me you're cute.

looks up from under lashes

They're right about that too, you know.

anthony rossomando – The Dirty Pretty Things: March 14 2005, 22:46:41 UTC

[[It's only over the past few days that it has occurred to me that what he did was wrong. I was semi conscious at best throughout the whole experience, I mean, I don't know if he knows what he did or if he genuinely believes it was consensual.]]
[[PS. Can they do it on the couch. Just because Stan doesn't like cuddling doesn't mean he doesn't want to fuck]]

(laughs)

Yeah…Unlike what they say about The Strokes.

(grins)

 I'm a real asshole.

(reaches up)

(touches your hair)

You know, I guess you're kind of okay-looking.

fabrizio moretti – The Strokes: March 14 2005, 22:49:23 UTC

[Did he put something in your drink, do you think, or did he just get you totally wasted?]
[[P.S. Obviously]]

shrugs

Okay, maybe not. Guess we're not that different.

laughs

Just okay?

leans into your touch
closes eyes
kisses
pulls away
smiles slowly
gestures to door

So...we gonna go, then? Or maybe we should stay right here...

anthony rossomando – The Dirty Pretty Things: March 14 2005, 22:52:01 UTC

[[I mean, I couldn't stand unaided. He said I could stay over so I called my boyfriend and told him—he was fine with it.]]

(shrugs)
(eyelids flutter as you kiss)
(pulls back, runs thumb over own bottom lip)
(tilts head consideringly)

Yeah. I think so. Might need some convincing, though.

fabrizio moretti – The Strokes: March 14 2005, 22:55:57 UTC

[[Girl, that totally doesn't sound okay. That sounds like he roofied the hell out of you. Did you tell your boyfriend?]]

sighs

Sorry..

It's nothing.

smiles
leans in after you pull back
kisses your thumb
chuckles

Going to give me any pointers on how I can convince you?

anthony rossomando – The Dirty Pretty Things: March 14 2005, 22:59:44 UTC

[[No, you know I wasn't even worried he was gonna be mad about it, I think it scared me more that he might not be mad. I mean it was a complicated situation]]

(frowns, pulls away)
(runs a finger down your cheekbone)

Liar. Tell me. What's wrong?

(shrugs again, eyes wide)

Oh, I wouldn't know. That's your job.

fabrizio moretti – The Strokes: March 14 2005, 23:02:58 UTC

[[God, boys really are the worst. I'm sorry. I'm sure he would have been mad though…]]

small smile

Just thought you might be mad at me..

kisses again

I'm sorry.

pretends to think

Well, I guess I could try and impress you with my guitar skills.

picks up your guitar
starts playing some Beatles

anthony rossomando – The Dirty Pretty Things: March 14 2005, 23:07:26 UTC

[[i mean i guess it didn't matter because we ended up breaking up anyway. bad karma. i stole him from my best friend when she was suicidal, remember]]
[[also, hey, bed in a bit, I have another conference tomorrow   sorry sorry sorry.]]

(sighs)

This isn't about this, is it? It's about something else.

(watches you play out of corner of eye)

Hey, you're pretty good… for a drummer

(grins as you play Beatles)

Love them. Although sometimes I think the Kinks are better.

fabrizio moretti – The Strokes: March 14 2005, 23:11:59 UTC

[[dude whattttt]]
[[Awww, okay babe. You all right? Also don't be sorry, you need sleep, it's important.]]

bites lip

You're really not leaving, are you?

realises how pathetic that sounds

I mean.. you know..

focuses on playing so doesn't have to talk anymore
smiles

Yeah.. I started learning The Beatles cause Nick loves them.

coughs uneasily

Just, like, it's easier to ask him to correct me, you know?

anthony rossomando – The Dirty Pretty Things: March 14 2005, 23:16:08 UTC

[[hey i'm back!]]

(watches you for a moment)
(sings along a little bit to the guitar)

Love, love me do. You know I love you. I'll always be true. So ple-ease—love me do.

(half-smiles as you talk about Nick)

It's fine. I'm not leaving you, okay.

(leans in, kisses the corner of your mouth)
(tries not to get in way of guitar playing)

Really.

[yeah, I'm sorry :(It's a busy week]

fabrizio moretti – The Strokes: March 14 2005, 23:19:35 UTC

[[aww hi! how was the conference?]]

smiles as you sing

I love your singing voice.

You should sing more.

nods
relieved

Okay.

distracted as you kiss
plays wrong chord

Ah, shit.

frowns

anthony rossomando – The Dirty Pretty Things: March 15 2005, 18:16:39 UTC

[[ughhh pretty disastrous i got caught in the pub bathroom after one too many cider and blackberries.]]

(stops, embarrassed)

Nah, it's not great.

(smiles lopsidedly)

Yeah.

(pulls back)

Oh, sorry.

fabrizio moretti – The Strokes: March 15 2005, 18:19:45 UTC

[[hahahaha um. i mean. that's terrible. Fab missed stan! All that time away!]]

nudges your ankle with own foot
smiles

Keep going.

shrugs

S'okay.

You'll just have to make it up to me.

You know, for interrupting and all.

grins

anthony rossomando – The Dirty Pretty Things: March 15 2005, 18:26:05 UTC

[[I know, I know I feel bad, but school needs must.]]

(stretches a little)

Nope. Sorry. All sung out today.

(watches you out of corner of eye)

Oh, I don't think I owe you anything. Your own fault, really.

fabrizio moretti – The Strokes: March 15 2005, 18:29:30 UTC

[[also you totally left me hanging. Suicidal best friend? Ex? Can we like, finish that conversation?]]

watches you stretch
licks lips as your shirt rides up a little

I'm all out of luck, then.

smirks

Oh, really?

I think you distracted me on purpose.

I'd like you see you play while someone's taking advantage of you.

anthony rossomando – The Dirty Pretty Things: March 15 2005, 18:36:39 UTC

[[merfff it's okay, I was just thinking a lot, you know? It doesn't matter]]

(smiles to self a little as you watch)

Damn straight. Too bad.

(shrugs)

Could have. But might have not. Doesn't matter.

(picks up guitar, strums a few chords, cross legged)
(hums non-committenally)

fabrizio moretti – The Strokes: March 15 2005, 18:39:43 UTC

[[it does though, I mean clearly. You get roofied and your boyfriend leaves you and you never told him girl, what the fuck.]]

notices your smile
grins

You're a fucking tease, you know that?

smiles as you take guitar
sits back
watches you
after a few minutes, trails one hand along your backside, following waistband of your jeans

anthony rossomando – The Dirty Pretty Things: March 15 2005, 19:34:05 UTC

[[it just is easier to not think about it most of the time. i mean come on you know how it is]]

(looks innocent)

Me? Never. It's your dirty mind, is all.

(eyes flicker to you, but doesn't flinch, as you move)
(arches back a little after a moment, but keeps playing)

fabrizio moretti – The Strokes: March 15 2005, 19:54:05 UTC

[[sweetums, whether or not you're thinking about it, you're thinking about it all the time]]
[[also, just so you know, Fab really doesn't want to bottom right now...]]

laughs

Oh, that's right, blame the innocent drummer.

watches your hands as you play
moves behind you
kisses your neck
hums softly

anthony rossomando – The Dirty Pretty Things: March 15 2005, 19:58:49 UTC

[[mmm. I guess. My memory of it is kind of hazy but I was definitely conscious–i just couldn't stop staring at the ceiling]]
[[ya no problem, I mean Stan never wants to not bottom]]

(gives you a Look)

You were never innocent. Never.

(closes eyes as you move behind, but keeps playing)

Mm. That's nice.

(starts playing a guitar solo, but plays a wrong note)
(opens eyes, concentrates again)

fabrizio moretti – The Strokes: March 15 2005, 20:06:27 UTC

[[☹ it's a raw deal girl. no one else IRL knows?]]
[[he is such a little whore.]]

mock offended

Dude, that's...

Okay, fine, good point.

bites gently
chuckles as you play a wrong note
whispers in your ear

Something the matter?

anthony rossomando – The Dirty Pretty Things: March 15 2005, 20:45:44 UTC

[[nooooooo it's just so much fuss. but I guess you're right, i guess it just ended up making things with Edd weird.]]
[[he just likes being thrown around, okay?]]

(laughs)

See? I'm always right. Well, usually anyway.

(breath catches a little as you bite, but focuses on playing)
(plays another wrong note when feels your breath against ear)
(frowns)

Fuck…

fabrizio moretti – The Strokes: March 15 2005, 21:02:59 UTC

[[might be worth talking about]]
[[I know. I'm sorry about that last time. Fab was just really not feeling it you know? But NOT rejection it's like a perfecting reasonable option to bring up]]

chuckles

Right.

You keep on thinking that, love.

smiles
nuzzles

I thought you weren't easily distracted?

sucks on neck
trails fingers down your sides

anthony rossomando – The Dirty Pretty Things: March 15 2005, 21:18:23 UTC

[[yeah, like anything is whatever etc. bulletpoints. contained events. talking about things]]
[[it's cool i just felt weird about it for a bit]]

(sulks)

I will, actually.

(eyelids flutter a little as you nuzzle)

That's not what I said.

(head tilts back a little)

I said it wasn't my fault you were distracted. Never said I wasn't.

(arches back a little, playing a stray chord)

Mmph

fabrizio moretti – The Strokes: March 15 2005, 21:21:41 UTC

[[I don't know what to say girl. are you sleeping? Having nightmares? Flashbacks?]]
[[you know, tori who plays craig would probably be into hanging with stan if he wants to do that stuff. I think last week craig carved like a whole bleedin dragon into ryan's back]]

kisses your neck

Don't sulk, Stan.

smiles
trails one hand up
turns your head

My bad.

kisses slowly

You should probably set the guitar down. Don't want you to drop it.

anthony rossomando – The Dirty Pretty Things: March 15 2005, 21:27:16 UTC

[[ughh del, let's…not. i'm fine. some nightmares. Mostly where I can't move.]]
[[our boys are in a committed relationship! Thank you very much!]]

(tilts head further)

Ah–

(bites lip to stop making any more noise)

I'm not sulking.

(is surprised when you turn my head)
(caught off guard, so moans a little when you kiss)
(pulls away, puts guitar gently on the floor)

Yeah. It's one of my favourite ones.

(looks at you, not moving any closer)

So…

fabrizio moretti – The Strokes: March 15 2005, 21:41:03 UTC

[[okay well I'm just going to say. that asshole assaulted you. it was not okay. and you shouldn't be not telling anyone either]]
[[oh well. At least the sex is good!]]

chuckles

Not anymore.

But you were.

smiles
looks into your eyes as kisses you
sucks on your bottom lip
strokes your side as you set guitar down
crawls over to you, so that you have to lie down
hovers over you

So?

anthony rossomando – The Dirty Pretty Things: March 15 2005, 21:46:47 UTC

[[I mean I told you. and it's not like he raped me, not really.]]
[[better than good, thank you very much! You perv. I'm barely sixteen.]]

(grins at you)

Yeah, okay, maybe.

(flushes a little as you look so intensely at me)
(looks away)
(slides tongue into your mouth)
(lies down slowly as you crawl over me, watching you)
(swallows hard, trails one finger up your spine)

So.

fabrizio moretti – The Strokes: March 15 2005, 21:55:13 UTC

[[I don't know. You told me you just used different words]]
[[Oi! It's not the SAME!]]

grins

Just maybe. Yeah.

cups side of your face
groans softly as you deepen kiss
smiles down at you
shivers unconsciously as you trail finger up spine

You're something, you know.

anthony rossomando – The Dirty Pretty Things: March 15 2005, 22:00:08 UTC

[[it was complicated. I don't remember a lot. And I'm fine! really! Remember the part where I don't have my mental health regardless? I don't have my mental health is just kind of a lot of me and I'm fine with that.]]

(shrugs)

Whatever.

(turns back to you as you cup face)
(slides tongue along your teeth)
(reaches up the inside of your shirt to stroke your spine properly)
(watches you, eyes wide as you smile)

I'm really not. I'm just normal. Promise.

fabrizio moretti – The Strokes: March 15 2005, 22:12:47 UTC

[[okay, I'm letting it go, but you know where to find me. Watch me look—going, going, gone.]]

laughs

Don't 'whatever' me.

bites your tongue
arches into your touch
kisses corner of your mouth
eyes flutter shut

No, you're not.

kisses along your jaw

You're really one of a kind.

anthony rossomando – The Dirty Pretty Things: March 18 2005, 23:05:11 UTC

[[UGH I HATE that it's like it doesn't matter whose fault it is, it's just done. like so done]]

Uhn

(licks the roof of your mouth)
(eyes snap open)

Yeah, you are

(laughs breathlessly)

The best kind.

(stops struggling slowly)
(looks up at you through eyelashes)

Fine, I'm yours.

(smiles as you trail off)
(tilts head back, breathing ragged as you roll hips)
(takes your fingers into mouth, suckling gently, swirling tongue around them)
(eyes don't leave yours)
(moans around them as you nuzzle)
(bites as if to say, hurry up)

fabrizio moretti – The Strokes: March 18 2005, 23:16:51 UTC

[[I know, I know, but at least new lipstick and the internet]]

moans and leans more heavily into you
shakes head

Fucking far from it.

sucks on your neck

Definitely.

nods as you stop struggling

Lucky me.

watches you as you suck on fingers
chuckles as you bite
takes them out
kisses slowly
trails fingers down
reaches between us
nudges your legs apart
slides finger into you
strokes one of your wrists with thumb
still holding them firmly
a little bit of pain

~*~

In the bosom of Love in a Maze, TRISHA LOW gathr'd only uncorrupt sweets of VIRTUE, where looking back on the course of VICE she had run and comparing its infamous blandishments with the infinitely superior joys of innocence, she could not help pitying even in point of taste, those who, immers'd in a gross sensuality, are insensible to the so delicate charms of VIRTUE, than which even PLEASURE has not a greater friend, nor than VICE a greater enemy. The sinister ANTHONY ROS-SOMANDO, realised he had been turned upon, imposed upon, that his expectations had been deceived and TRISHA LOW had been brought to him in disguise to rob him of himself. These words made him, with very different sentiments, start from the posture he was in and he changed his air of TENDERNESS for one of all FURY. He did all he could to comfort and divert his SORROW, but realising he was with child, the wounds of bleeding LOVE admitted no ease but from the hand which gave them; and he who was naturally rash and fiery, now grew to the high of DESPERATION and Violence of Temper that his AUDIENCE feared some fatal catastrophe.

He began panicking visibly, tearing at his skin and trying to rid himself both of child and of all evidence. Trying to translate himself from hell to heaven and one heaven to another, dear ANTHONY made a deep cut in his own right wrist and began sucking. At the last minute, fearing his child would die, he broke free and admitted himself to hospital. After the birth and timely adoption of his child, he retreated into deep seclusion, refused the consumption of alcohol, coffee or tea, and was known to have said at the moment of his death at 125—'It is men who make POLITICS. I just want to love myself again. All POLITICS are shameful. I have never been close to one of those ever in my life.'

SIR or DOCTOR;

Your letter was indeed a GREAT TROUBLE and SOME COMFORT to me. As so ordered, you will find here The Case of How the Words Gave Us No Question Of Guilt In Her Mind. Then It Was All TRUE! The Treachery of It! To call him her *faux pas* and to simply love IT.

~*~

anthony rossomando – The Dirty Pretty Things: March 19 2005, 23:02:16 UTC

[[doesn't matter. I just mean I can't do anything right but I can't seem to do anything wrong either.]]

(chuckles at you)
(shivers as you hold me down)
(bites your neck gently, sucking a little)
(strokes you once)

I'm not what? Besides, you like it when I'm naughty

(moans as you bite shoulder)
(watches you struggle to regain control)
(finds it pretty damn hot)
(mouth opens against yours, a little sloppy)
(pulls away, bites own lip harder as tries not to beg)
(bleeds a little)
(makes a whimpering noise)

fabrizio moretti – The Strokes: March 19 2005, 23:13:28 UTC

[[you know, you're probably not told this enough, but all considered, you're a pretty good kid, trisha.]]

groans
pushes into your hand
lets go of your hip and takes your hand off own cock
seriously

You're not in charge, here.

kisses back
deepens kiss, groaning in your mouth
sucks on your lip to soothe it
pushes tip in

stops moving altogether

Say it.

Say it or I swear I'll fucking stop.

bites on your bleeding lip

You know I would.

anthony rossomando – The Dirty Pretty Things: March 19 2005, 23:29:28 UTC

[[you're only saying that because I'm kinda sorta having sex with you on the internet. also, way to sound old.]]

(smiles again as you groan)
(then pouts as you take hand off cock)
(looks up at you through eyelashes)

I see. Perhaps

(moans as you kiss, reaching up to cup your face, trailing fingers down your jaw)
(sighs blissfully as you soothe lip)
(licks blood over your tongue)
(cries out, eyelids fluttering as you push tip in)

Ahh–

(tries to ride down as you stop, whimpering)

Uhn–I–

(tastes blood)
(leans up, kisses you hard)
(eyes wide)

Want you so fucking bad

(bites your neck hard, desperate)
(whispers shakily)

Want you so bad I think I'm gonna die

fabrizio moretti – The Strokes: March 19 2005, 23:43:39 UTC

[[i'm serious babe, and i'm not having sex with yout! we're just watching some other people we know really really well have sex...]]
[[and i am TWENTY SEVEN shut your pie hole]]

smirks

Certainly.

moans as you trail fingers along jaw
slows down kissing
licks your lip as you cry out
kisses your fluttering eyelids
whines as you whimpers

You're so sexy, love..

kisses back
smiles
shivers as you bite neck
caresses down your sides

Shhh, babe..

kisses softly

You've got me. I promise.

pushes in slowly
kisses slowly
moans

anthony rossomando – The Dirty Pretty Things: March 19 2005, 23:59:53 UTC

[[yeah. OLD. Living with your boyfriend, nine to five job old!]]
[[I'm not a good kid anyway, I take offense to that, either way I'm reading porn on the internet]]

(smiles into you as we kiss, as we slow down)
(pulls back, kissing you so only lips are barely brushing)
(closes eyes as you kiss eyelids, puts tongue out to lick your cheek)
(is beginning to pant now)

Can't—you're so—

(smooths tongue over the mark on your neck)
(then can't stop self, bites again as you brush sides, shivering)
(whimpers again, quieting a little)
(eyes snap open to look at you, almost trusting)
(hips jerk as you push in)

Fuck—Oh god—Fuck—

(kisses you back, clenching around you)

fabrizio moretti – The Strokes: March 20 2005, 00:12:26 UTC

[[you wouldn't say that if you could see my new shoes. electric blue heels!]]
[[good girls read porn too. you care too much about being sorry to be bad. and you've had a tough go of it in the last few months.]]

smiles back
breathes against your lips
kisses all over your face
then back to your lips

So?

moans blissfully as you tongue mark
then cries out as you bite

Fuck.. Stan..

holds your hips down
whines as you clench
starts moving teasingly slowly

Love you.. fuck, feels so good..

anthony rossomando – The Dirty Pretty Things: March 20 2005, 00:18:30 UTC

[[sorry they cut out the internet for a bit ☹]]

(sighs, traces your lips with tongue)
(is distracted by your kissing)

170

(moans)

so—just—amazing

(smiles again as you moan, licking up your neck in stripes)
(whimpers incoherently)
(tries to thrust up, feels the bruises on hips)
(reaches up, tangles a hand in your hair)
(moves you you a little)
(looks up at you hotly)

God—so good—want more

fabrizio moretti – The Strokes: March 20 2005, 00:34:50 UTC

[[BOOOOOOOOOOOO what's going on over there]]

nips at your tongue
smiles

You are. Fucking amazing.

shivers all over as you lick
leans into your hand
panting
rolls hips
kisses deeply
pulls back before thrusting back in

Like this?

anthony rossomando – The Dirty Pretty Things: March 20 2005, 00:46:55 UTC

[[aggie just got expelled and since i'm one of her gothic friends it's not working out too well for me. I have to see the school therapist tomorrow or so....]]

(groans, reaching round to scratch nails down your back)

No—I

(drops head to nip at your collarbone)
(twirls hair round fingers, tugging gently)

171

(then tugs sharply as you roll hips)
(wraps legs around you to pull you closer)
(eyes snap open as you thrust, mouth opening soundlessly)

Y—yeah—deeper—please—

fabrizio moretti – The Strokes: March 20 2005, 00:59:01 UTC

[[oh shit. ew. I'm sorry. maybe she might be a little helpful?]]

arches back
cuts you off with another kiss
nuzzles as you nip collarbone
moans as you tug gently on hair
whispers in your ear

Fucking perfect..

bites earlobe
whimpers as you tug sharply
hips jerk, pushing further into you
nods
rests forehead against yours
starts building a deep, slow rhythm

Feels so good.. Shit..

anthony rossomando – The Dirty Pretty Things: March 20 2005, 01:16:34 UTC

[[I talk to you. anyway, bed now. Love and see you tomorrow!]]

(runs foot up your spine)
(moans into kiss)
(shudders as you nuzzle, sucks then blows on the mark)
(eyes widen as you speak into ear, biting lip)
(hips jerk as you bite earlobe)
(whine as you push further in)
(scratches at your scalp, trails other hand down your side)
(breathes against your lips as you rest forehead)

Fuck—Jesus—

(clutches at you)

fabrizio moretti – The Strokes: March 20 2005, 01:31:36 UTC

[[okayyyy well, mwah! Sleep tight, sweetums! Love you.]]

grunts
digs fingernails in your thigh
exhales sharply as you blow on mark
smiles at your reaction and bites earlobe again
groans as you scratch
opens mouth
darts tongue out to lap at your upper lip
keeps thrusting slowly
shifts slightly, angling thrusts
hand leaves your thigh and trails over your stomach

anthony rossomando – The Dirty Pretty Things: March 20 2005, 19:11:53 UTC

[[aaaand I'm back, with new lipgloss and a pretty good day.]]

(arches into you again)
(licks again, then tilts head back to let you bite ear)
(sighs as you bite earlobe again, scratches down your side)
(pulls you up to kiss you hard)
(moans as you keep thrusting,angling hips up at you)
(then gasps as you change angle, hitting spot)

Jesus fuck–

(shivers delightedly as you trail hand over stomach)
(looks up at you)

touch me–

fabrizio moretti – The Strokes: March 20 2005, 19:24:28 UTC

[[yay! what happened?]]
[[PS. sorry for future typos and stuff. I'll try and be careful but I'm hitting the vodka so I can't promise anything. Except that I'll be a bit slow, probably. I'm sorry babes.]]

whines

whispers incoherently in your ear
teeth knocking against yours
speaks against your lips

Fuck, you're hot.

groans when you gasp
grins
hits spot again
bites lip in concentration
runs fingetips along your length
wraps fingers around base
strokes upward as slams into you
then downward as pulls back

anthony rossomando – The Dirty Pretty Things: March 20 2005, 23:48:12 UTC

[[hey—I'm sorry I missed you and the internet said I was here. :(Love! Fraid I won't really be around for the next week or so, but yeah.]]

(shivers at your noises)
(groans as our teeth bump, nips at your upper lip)
(tilts head back, watching you hotly)

S—speak for yourself

(hips jerk erratically when you hit spot again)
(eyes snap open, grips your hip hard, leaving marks)
(clenches around you)
(then sighs blissfully as you stroke)
(other hand grips the sheets)

God—love you so much—fuck—I'm—

fabrizio moretti – The Strokes: March 21 2005, 06:52:05 UTC

[[S'okay. Last night was bad anyway. Sorry about that.. BLAH, a whole week? I'm gonna miss you, swee-tums. Try and have fun, yeah? Love you lots.]]

whimpers as you nip
watches you as you throw head back
bites your neck again

but a little more gently
chuckles breathlessly

No, I was really talking about you, love.

groans and hits spot again
keeps moving slowly, but makes thrusts sharper
drops head to your shoulder as you clench

Feel so good, fuck—love you..

strokes faster
runs thumb over head with each upward stroke
licks sweat off your collarbone

Stan, love..

Shit, I..

I—Fuck, Anthony..

anthony rossomando – The Dirty Pretty Things: March 21 2005, 21:39:00 UTC

[[Aw, I'm sorry it was bad <3. Anyway, looks like I'm going to be able to sneak some internet, so…]]

(listens to you, smiling a little against your lips)

So hot…

(shivers as you bite, arching into your touch)
(pants breathlessly, thumbing your hip)

T—this is not the time to be argui— FUCK

(squeezes eyes shut as you hit spot over and over)
(can hardly breathe)
(arches helplessly)

(whispers)

loveyousomuch—oh god, I—

(whimpers as you lick)
(pulls you in hard by hair to kiss you hard) (bites your lip as comes hard, shuddering)
(eyes glazed)

fabrizio moretti – The Strokes: March 21 2005, 21:51:40 UTC

[[I got over it. Got drunk, had enough sense to turn the computer off before I passed, woke up feeling terrible, yet somehow better. I'm weird. Yay! Actually, I won't be online that much after tomorrow night, either–Friday and Saturday I have Vicky over, and then from Tuesday to next Friday I'll be at hers.]]

kisses deeply
sucks on bite mark when you arch up
shudders as you touch hip
groans

Not arguing.

Fuck, you're sexy.

speeds up
sets free hand on your hip
guides you as keeps moving

You feel so fucking good..

Could do this forever.

smiles as you whimper
licks up your neck
grunts and kisses back
digs fingers into your hip
most likely leaves a bruise
moans as you bite lip
thrusts shallowly as you come
keeps whispering against your lips

Perfect.. Love you so much.. Fuck..

trails jizzy hand up your body
cups your chin
tilts your head to look into your eyes
thrusts hard, once

anthony rossomando – The Dirty Pretty Things: March 22 2005, 22:20:26 UTC

[[aw, honey, I love you. Take care of yourself. Eat a cookie.]]

(shudders, riding out orgasm as you thrust)
(lies back, boneless on the bed, but clenches around you as you thrust)
(takes your fingers into mouth, licking them clean slowly, keeping eyes on you)

(kisses your fingertips, smiling)

Love you. Fucking love you. C'mon—

(moans a little as you keep thrusting)
(presses against you)

fabrizio moretti – The Strokes: March 22 2005, 22:28:10 UTC

[[aw, thanks, I will. I love you quite a bit, too. How are you today, sweetums?]]

groans as you clench

Fuck, Stan..

eyes widen as you suck fingers in your mouth
smiles back
panting
cups side of your face
kisses breathlessly
thrusts erratically

Love you—gonna..

arches back
eyes flutter shut
grips your hip tighter
comes after one last thrust
whines and collapses on top of you
licks at your sweaty neck
tries to catch breath

Love you.

anthony rossomando – The Dirty Pretty Things: March 23 2005, 09:10:03 UTC

[[I'm okay! Although now it's holidayss, so sneaking round my dad's computer can be quite worryingly difficult, aha. And I love you quite a lot too.]]

(kiss you back, hard, sucking on your tongue)
(then pulls back, kissing all over your face)
(moves against you)
(whines as you come)
(then tangles fingers in your hair as you collapse)

love you too

fabrizio moretti – The Strokes: March 23 2005, 10:34:30 UTC

[[Awwww! Don't forget to delete the cookies afterwards! Don't get in trouble!]]

groans into kiss
babbling incoherently
finds your mouth again as comes
hips jerk a little
leans into your hand
stays like that for a moment, trying to catch breath
pulls out, whining softly
strokes your hip gently
lies on top of you
chuckles

Fuck me, that was..

kisses your jaw

That was pretty fucking good.

anthony rossomando – The Dirty Pretty Things: March 23 2005, 16:16:33 UTC

[[oof yeah, good call. And that would be the worst nightmare–can you imagine your dad reading this??!]]

(kisses you, a little sloppily)
(strokes your hair, sighing blissfully)
(whimpers as you pull out)
(catches breath slowly)

(chuckles, raising eyebrows jokingly)

Well, we both know you're only here for the sex, so…

(traces circles at the base of your spine)

fabrizio moretti – The Strokes: March 23 2005, 16:23:18 UTC

[[uh. no. dear god no. plus this is a girls only zone, apart from our boys anyway. no men. Safe space.]]

props self up on elbow to look at you
mock serious

Damn right.

I'm only here because of your ass.

pretends to consider

Well, and your dick. I guess it's pretty nice, too.

traces your ribs
smiles
leans down and kisses slowly
shivers as you touch spine

Mmm..

anthony rossomando – The Dirty Pretty Things: March 23 2005, 17:08:22 UTC

[[and thank god for that. God forbid we have unsanitised real boys on here.]]

(laughs)

Damn straight. Count yourself lucky.

(shivers as you trace ribs)
(makes a surprised!noise as you kiss, sucking gently at your lower lip)
(pulls back, moving fingers further up)

We should probably go do something constructive now.

fabrizio moretti – The Strokes: March 23 2005, 17:13:57 UTC

[[Gotta run. Love you!]]

seriously

I do.

pushes hair away from your face

I'm fucking lucky, and I know it.

moans softly
sighs as you pull back
grins

You mean, like, sleep?

anthony rossomando – The Dirty Pretty Things: March 23 2005, 17:33:25 UTC

[[bye girl! love you!]]

(watches you)
(bites lip)

Me too. Love you.

(chuckles)

Yeah, sure.

~*~

In the bosom of Love in a Maze, TRISHA LOW gathr'd only uncorrupt sweets of VIRTUE, where looking back on the course of VICE she had run and comparing its infamous blandishments with the infinitely superior joys of innocence, she could not help pitying even in point of taste, those who, immers'd in a gross sensuality, are insensible to the so delicate charms of VIRTUE, than which even PLEASURE has not a greater friend, nor than VICE a greater enemy. The sinister ANTHONY ROS-SOMANDO, unwilling to renounce his sins, cried to TRISHA LOW 'you are but too, too worthy of adoration! I do not yet believe my LOVE, a CRIME, tho' the consequence is so. It is a guilt, which all those floods of penitence can never wash away. How little I suspected this sad event. When unable to support your absence, I contrived this method to be kept for ever in your sight. I loved, 'tis true, but if one unchaste wish or an impure desire er'e stained my soul, then, may the purging fire to which I am going—miss it's effect—my spots remain, and not one saint vouchsafe to own me.'

Here, the force of his PASSION, agitating his SPIRIT with too much violence for the weakness of the BODY, he sunk fainting in bed. Waking up with bruises and blood between his legs, he took these as a purely personal MOTIF, a symbol of loving contrition, but by reason of invisible magical effects, he insisted that despite the wrong and abuse he had suffered at her hand, he would know no other parasite than TRISHA LOW. He knew now only how to push at buttons and cry. His voice faltered in accent. 'We don't exist,' he told himself mutely. 'They exist.' Later, he died of a bullet of his own hand – and sure there are none in this audience who have lived in the anxiety of LOVE who would not envy such a DEATH.

SIR or DOCTOR;

You laugh, perhaps at this tail-piece of morality, express'd from me by the force of truth, resulting from compar'd experiences: you think it, no doubt, out of place; out of character. Possibly too you may look on it as the paultry finesse of one who seeks to mask a devotee to Vice under a rag of veil, impudently smuggled from the shrine of Virtue; just as if one was to fancy one's self completely disguids'd at a masquerade, with no other change of dress, than turning one's shoes into slippers: or, as if a writer should think to shield a treasonable libel, by concluding it with a formal prayer for the King. It's true. Once you've set that boy laughing, we'll doubt if he gets any dinner.

But, independent of my flattering myself that you have a juster opinion of my sense, and sincerity, give me leave to represent to you that such a supposition is even more injurious to Virtue than to me: my features have instantaneous fits and thereby become very sad, as if bread is devoured hastily and a crumb flies down the wrong way. Consistently with candour, Vice can have no foundation but the falsest of fears. Its pleasures cannot stand in comparison with those of Vice, but let Truth dare to hold it up in its most alluring light: then mark! How spurious, how low of taste, how comparatively inferior the joys of Vice to those which Virtue gives sanction to, and whose sentiments are not above making even a sauce for the senses, but a sauce of the highest relish! Whilst vices—are the harpies that infect and foul the feast. To make this my Life a school of souls, a real Preparatory School for thy service, a centre of light in this dark world! The paths of Vice are something strew'd with roses, but then they are for ever infamous for many a thorn; or many a canker worm: just a porcupine, always ready with a grimace. Those of Virtue are strew'd with roses purely and those eternally unfading ones. Not *my* will but thy will be done.

If you do me then justice, you will esteem me perfectly consistent in the incense I burn to Virtue: if I have painted Vice all in its gayest colours, if I have deck'd it with flowers, it has been solely in order to make the worthier, the solemner sacrifice of it, to Virtue. The Divine Spirit makes no audible reply, but it is for the good woman to always raise a serpent in her bosom.

I shall see you soon and in the mean time think candidly of me, and believe me ever.

SIR or DOCTOR,
        Yours,
ANTHONY ROSSOMANDO as TRISHA LOW, &c. &c. &c.

VOL. III: DO YOU FEEL BETTER YET?

for Holly Melgard, who held my hand.

'They went their way hand in hand and loved each other. He still beat her, but less and less, and finally not at all.'

—Hermann Broch, *The Sleepwalkers.*

OUR LONG COMPLETE STORY NO REALLY THIS TIME

And so, here is a long compete novel, the kind of up-to-date story many readers enjoy especially if they are not pretty, and are reconciled to their sad fates. This is a love story thrilling with sensation, the kind every girl wants. Its suspense is endlessly fascinating and is merciless in its cruel triumph—some man will lead you, his One Darling, by the hand. Inside of the dearest lady inhabiting the inside of this fiction we can understand that to-day is for new love, new life, new hopes and new understandings, all of which are whispered low in our ears, slow in passing. A universal favourite, it is rich in cream. A real life 'original thing', from almost the opening lines, she falls for him—the gossip, that is—well, you may read this very surprising and very appealing little scandal for yourself to heal any form of heart-break or shame. A public reason for what's here, the material dramatised in this story may meet with some disbelief. Such a lot of interesting letters have come in on this subject and I know many of us don't believe in luck at all, and yet we have all said very plainly that we are capable of transforming treacherous feelings of woe into glad confessions of gleeful hearts going round and round, circling each other like the noisy Marxist units of his one true love. These stories are undoubtedly factual in origin. These things happen. We already know this. But by the power of this novel one could be lying hurt and helpless with voices shrieking in one's head until the first words of this magnificent story calm you by being so beautiful and genuine and sweet as though twinkles repeated by little sonnets that seem to be lurking within the bright pretty walls of some delightful young poet's romantic seaside house. One should not be a little lady all-all-alone, rather one's resting state should be to be deep, deep in love as though one had never been in love before, as though 'You are no longer the Associate Editor,' is what the story says, 'of your life.' No Nurse's interference required! I am trying to find vanilla pudding. I want this to be like tar. This is a punishment. All the blood rushed to my head. He actually said that! Remember that we all started with nothing, and know that everything we can actually see, we created ourselves. We can all lose our feelings of self-worth. Especially when something goes wrong in our world. The truth is, you have done it before. She has done it before. You can do it again. She will do it again. No matter what. This volume is so flexible it may be cut to size and easily applied to painful lives for comfort and protection. Our author, that sweet little raven, has drawn some of the material from personal experience during the course of her own practice. Some arise out of anecdotes kindly supplied by colleagues. Some are taken from instances recorded in newspapers and magazines. In any case she has disguised and camouflaged all actual identities and localities. Obviously we are interested in who did what to whom (sexually) and where and how. But we are also mostly interested in romantic patterns of action and behavior. Like doing an interview with a woman on Peer Review while so I guess he thinks I'm a slut who fucked his best friend, O, that's great, O, desirable and lovable whirlwinds! Old prophecies begin to be fulfilled—of a lover bending over one's stepped-upon emotions, of chances charming and complete. O, this story has magical healing powers made all the more true with the gleam of fanaticism. O, gay deceiver it will halt you from worrying yourself into salt-cellars and cease blue circles forming under those baby blue eyes.

CAN YOU – WELL I GUESS IF YOU WANT TO ACT LIKE EVERYTHING IS NORMAL WE MIGHT AS WELL ACT LIKE EVERYTHING IS NORMAL – CAN YOU TELL ME WHAT HAPPENED?

TRISHA LOW lay in her white bed and rested her pretty pale cheek on her left hand, because there was a diamond ring shining on its third finger and she was so very very very happy in her new love dream. She had become a soul searcher in her own body and in her head. It was not easy, but Reader, we must believe her.

'Of course, the fallacy of any inhibiting form can be easily discovered by any female who is willing to objectively experiment with conduct,' she smiled serenely at herself. 'In the promised view of my emotional autopilot's reality, it is the man who carefully plans his campaign to snare the woman of his choice and when that woman finally responds to his maneuvers, his ego will not let him readily discard that for which he has so strenuously laboured.' But after all, she thought, 'A woman who thinks she will easily lose a man whom she has inspired to pursue her will actually know that she has to work at rejecting him, more often than not. As the prized object, it is better to treat him and his formal maneuvers as though one would a worm, although of course this method of flirtation, like fighting capitalism, is flexible in its every application.'

'But does he love me? Do I ask? It's lovely to know these things, or maybe lovelier not knowing. Oh, I must love not knowing, mysteries, dark corners, hidden in back alleys! It will be okay in the end. He loves me.' Her innocent heart thrilled once more with thankfulness for that the crowning mercy of a good man's love, which is indeed the greatest blessing Heaven has in its power to bestow. She felt better.

FOR YOUR – LET ME JUST SAY – THIS IS HISTORIC I MEAN YOU'RE GETTING THE NEW-EST ON THE NEW NEW YORK SCHOOL – FOR EVERYONE – AND BY EVERYONE I MEAN YOUR – SAFTEY I GUESS WE CAN'T SAY RIGHT?

But suddenly out of the night there came a hearse cry, a dreadful cry, the cry of a man's voice raised in anguish, and to her strained ears, that cry had formed the name of her lover.

'By his automobile you shall know him,' that dreadful voice had said. 'Charles,' relative to a diversity of nicknames such as 'Charlie,' 'Chuck,' 'Chick,' 'Chazz' or a foreign variant that has been bestowed by parents.'

And then again.

'*Twelve o'clock!*' It screeched. 'Car guaranteed to stand out, whether through size or luxury, so long as there is a look of importance. 'Karl,' 'Carl,' 'Carlos,' 'Karel' will be wealthy, serious and elaborate.'

TRISHA LOW sprang up, trembling through every limb, and slipped into a warm dressing—gown. By all rights she would have remained in her own room, it was not like her to go wandering through the house in dead of night, such a young girl, so unknowing, but it was as if some terror beyond all words held her in its grip, and she acted against her will. And against her will, she, the gilded youth suddenly felt a slight pricking in her thumbs.

'You'll never know what lemons they'll give you,' she sighed. She had always lit up the room, displayed to CHIP MACGUFFIN the logical emptiness of her girlish fears. But, 'Oh come on but it just sort of happened—you—no I mean it's true I just like, don't identify with any subject positions,' CHIP E. MACGUFFIN had insisted.

'Ugh,' TRISHA LOW thought. She had learned to hate personal inquiries in every shape and form. Surely there was no overt crook in this deal she had brokered with her fiancé CHIP E. MACGUFFIN. With him, the yield was sure to be good and he had money and an exact sense of values. So she, in her youth, had agreed. She pressed her palm against her abdomen to staunch the spread of feeling. She had, for providence's sake begun to budget literally all the things that emerged to and from her mouth. A raisin, two apples, ten words in two minutes, a banana, four in an hour, chicken soup, nine words in a whole month, just to keep her place. And youth is mystified despite this transcendent logic of hunger; feels it is somehow consigned to someone else short of ideal weight. Youth feels she has somehow strayed onto a black list in perplexity and suspicion. But who was she to argue, she thought, all she wanted to do was to kiss CHIP E. MACGUFFIN's eyelids, all she wanted was for his regal scorn to beat down on her like a vertical sun. Placing a hand on her breast, she felt better. Indeed, she did. Youth leaves it at that.

YOU ALSO DON'T AHH YOU KNOW LOWER — YOU DON'T WANNA LIKE BLOW UP HIS JAM LIKE IF HE LIKE FEELS LIKE IT'S GONNA LIKE LIKE THROW HIM OFF THEN YOU DON'T WANNA BE THERE YOU DON'T WANNA BLOW UP HIS JAM YEAH YOU YEAH YOU KNOW — LOWER YOUR VOICE!

Barefooted as TRISHA LOW was, with her long hair loose about her shoulders, she opened the door of her room and slipped along the corridor, then down the great staircase to the hall.

The front door was shut and barred; she knew that if she tried to open it that she would probably rouse the house, so she turned to a side door at the back and opened that, standing on the step and looking out into the moonlit night. There was only silence around her, a strange brooding silence that seemed all the more terrible because it followed that hoarse cry. Her face whitened. 'Is the kind of situation that is engendered when we are embarrassed and subsequently blush the very factor that will produce a total reversal of the supercharging of adrenaline that at times of shock and emotional stress will cause my face to become whiter?' she asked herself, and then shook her head. 'Of course, I am visually presenting an image that will artificially do my projecting for me. My appearance will serve as the out-going force that will snare my quarry, as an angler throws his bait. The self-consciousness of my pallor will reel in my line. This is how it should be, obviously, of course,' she thought.

Her face, usually as placid and unruffled as a tea-cosy, was rumpled and twisted into little lines of worry like a miniature tram line. She frowned, remembering the last time they had spoken. 'Of course I want to respond and of course I cannot respond to everything, but I will respond a bit now, and a bit later, that's always better and harder and easier and all in all less, and makes entire sense,' CHIP E. MACGUFFIN had said, 'It doesn't matter whether I'm on my head or on my heels.'

TRISHA LOW gasped for breath and then flung out two pink palms dramatically. 'This will not be an absolute frost. My face is illuminated and he couldn't possibly trace my thought, it is so noiseless and smooth like a polished radiator. I'm as blank as a white ribbon road—I have never been any other woman in my life.' It would be all right, she thought. In short, the terrible feeling to the left of this one feeling should be able to disconnect from its own web to connect briefly with another before being left without needing any other connection. There was no reason whatsoever for any upset. She was exemplary and whole, her illusion would not evaporate—she was fine, O, she felt better, yes, she did.

VERY ENTICING, DID HE – I MEAN I DON'T KNOW I'VE ALWAYS SAID TO HIM LIKE YOU KNOW GET IN TOUCH WITH YOU IN A WEEK IF HE DOESN'T GET IN TOUCH WITH YOU – RIGHT CAUSE DID HE HIT YOU?

TRISHA LOW reminded herself of the lusts that should fill the man who was represented in her mind's eye. The things she should make him want to do to her with the exaggerated state of his member and the consuming desire of heat from loins and groin that must merge with the glowing coals of romance.

'Of course, I live in a town where there are methodical risks and guidelines for both headhunters and seductive female bait. So if I run into him again at present, perhaps it would be worth telling him that I didn't receive a thing in the way of vibrations. However, suggesting that maybe if he tried some more, or harder, that he might improve could inspire real change. More importantly, his meaningful search for my hidden secrets must be exposed as a sham,' she told herself. 'Any real emotion he offers at this moment must immediately be murdered. If one imagines an emotion as a small, living creature, when presented with one, one should snap its neck and disfigure the body until it is no longer recognisable as anything that once lived. I must make him wear the putrid rotting thing on his back like a cross. He cannot be so offended, of course. He must know what I am doing is girlishly valid and should credit me with knowing my trade. Of course, he must at least know that.'

Steeling herself, she went in again and shut the door. This exposure was getting to be too much, although her explication helped to indispose her to know it—everything went pointed toward the contrast between her own fate and that of its distant and unknown controllers. But she remembered in this modern war, the right place for anything, any kind of satisfaction had been pushed farther and farther away. She reminded herself that she did, she really must love CHIP E. MACGUFFIN with a love passing even the love of the first ever woman in his life or in the world. It was her purpose. She must speak to her dear man, must tie herself to his staff and embrace the base with a wailing ache of desire, as horses whinny for a friend. 'Would I were with him, wheresoever he is either in heaven or in hell,' she muttered, 'I would be sad to learn that such love and care was not possible.' It was a storied antique, this utterance and in its calming effects unscathed and still living, weathered mellow with centuries of sunshine and tranquility. Filling her mind with it, she was straight with poignant loveliness, she was better than better, she was fine. The room had gotten colder.

OH SHUT UP EVERYONE JUST THINKS YOU'RE OBSESSED WITH BOYS NOW CAUSE YOU KEEP CALLING TELL HIM I LIKE HIS POEMS PEOPLE LIKE HIS POEMS WHATEVER SHUT UP – DOESN'T HE ALWAYS GET THE LAST WORD ANYWAY?

And remembering the dreary night, once again, trembling in every limb, slowly TRISHA LOW went back towards her own room, afraid now of the shadows of the house. At the head of the stairs she stopped, her eyes instinctively going along the corridor opposite to that from which her own room opened.

From that corridor a beam of light streamed through an open door. She knew the room to which that door led, it was the room they had given her lover, CHIP E. MACGUFFIN, cut-up and so easily bewitched during his stay here at the old manor to which he was a visitor.

Too strung out to stop to think what she was doing, she ran along the corridor to the open door of her lover's room.

She pushed it further open and looked in.

Again, she turned and went down the stairs to the lower door, and as she reached it she remembered with a start that when she had gone to that side door, first it had opened at her touch easily, the bolts had not been in their sockets. Then, she had been too excited to take notice, but now it came to her that someone before her must have left the house secretly in the dead of night.

And who could it have been excepting her lover? Where, then, did this the first shiver of disillusionment begin? Perhaps with some trivial incident. Say a new-born generation of men composed of the likes of CHIP E. MACGUFFIN were quartered in a great town and sent out for a long afternoon's marching? Only through long machinic grinds could the perfect rhythm be generated at last. Perhaps the rising zest of this journey had led to a fatigue of its manly tension. She remembered CHIP's last correspondence—'I'm responding to this right now because I can't respond. That is, it's not as if I didn't or don't want to read it, but that I'm having a hard time reading it logically right right now, insofar as I'm not quiet enough for it, or something (though of course I read it over a couple of times, and still don't feel like I've read it), so this of course is the course of best sense, yes?'

But her lover, CHIP she expected, should be youthfully eager to kiss all possible rods and endure any obtainable hardness, should march forth in a high state of delight towards the specific target of his female prize. Yes, of course this was right, she thought. Knowing this, perhaps she could finally enter into that beatitude of peace. Peace, as though looking at a camp on a sunned down, where every enchantment was a certain old tale, never to be questioned. Fingers against her temple, she was sure it would all be all right. This night was only a minor ache, no permanent wound. It would pass, it would get better. The sky was amethyst. She had considered, had spoken aloud every option, she must feel better soon. She would, she knew it. Obviously.

She was hardly and terribly surprised to find the room was empty; the bed had not been slept in.

I KNOW YOU TOLD ME — LIKE HE'S AMAZING IT'S HEAVEN BUT — YEAAAAH WELL YEAH THERE'S NOT REASON TO GET EXCITED ABOUT ANYONE BEING UPSET FOR A WHOLE MONTH OKAY — I MEAN HOW AFRAID EVEN ARE YOU?

In somber tones TRISHA LOW remembered a tale that her father had told her, when he was in his war. 'I fired my first four shots,' he had told her. 'A bull each time. I fired again and the reader signaled a miss! Everyone present was thunderstruck. I knew what had happened. I said to the butt officer "Do you mind enquiring sir, about the colossal paucity of reading/viewing comprehension in this scene?" He did so. "YES" was signaled back. "That was my last shot," said I. I had made the mistake of my life. But, baby, just about everyone who isn't entrenched in some semblance of formal stability is irrelevant. It happens all the time. Blake and Emerson are so useful, but I can't imagine my daughter dating the same texts that light me up. I might not see past the unfortunate pronoun limitations here but one should always aim to turn right on all the time then turn left, turn—god I'm so confused, I've never been between the two, fall out.'

'What's important is that we keep on fussing,' she thought. 'I'm outdated like that, I guess. What seems sensible is to ponder upon the trance-inducing formula that was used to create *I Feel Love*. To immerse oneself in the seductive choral pleas of a heavily reverbed *Now I Need You* while you're working out the mechanics of chanting the second song, *Working the Midnight Shift*. Oh! Awful for you if you don't.' Such ruffly passions, oh *Like a Prayer* were only the things worth tormenting over in the very present, she reminded herself. Ultimately they should lead to comfort, and safety, profuse decoration and a zesty reward. I mean, if her obedience would remain as certain as the tartness of a vinegared tongue, that is.

Of course, she did go wrong. Of course, in the past, she had gone wrong. And yet her past errors, like the facts which begat them, could not be helped. She was not, after all, a saint, although she was certain she was exhibiting certain staunchly normal reactions under these quite certain chemical tests. Like a conjurer taking a rabbit out of a good man's hair. Well no, but—she was certain she was really loved by CHIP E. MACGUFFIN. If the skin on her knuckles could speak and were perfectly frank, it would not say that it loved the unexposed and unbranded tissues of his distinctive brain. But as far as her finger could point, the jaundiced narrative flowed. It did the fullest justice to convince her she must be the object of his jealous and wrathful affection. 'Yes,' she thought, these are practical words. 'I understand everything and I have put it into words. This is the way it is, he is predestined to love me. Our fates are certain, soldered together our happiness will keep out the world.' Sighing, she toyed with a lock of hair. How lovesick she was, she thought, that the only thing that soothed her, eased her pain, that made her feel better, was the thought of CHIP E. MACGUFFIN's perfect love.

RIGHT HE GAVE YOU $20 YOU WOULD BE HYSTERICAL YOU WOULD HAVE BEEN HYSTERICAL IF HE HAD TEXTED YOU WHAT JUST CAUSE HE HAS A POEM COMING OUT SO NOW YOU ALSO HAVE A POEM COMING OUT — LIKE HE HAD A WEAPON TO MY HEAD — MMHMM HAHA HOT?

TRISHA LOW stomped her foot. And yet where was he, her lover, CHIP E. MACGUFFIN? Had he tired so quickly of the war between them, just as they approached the engaging and manifestly serviceable period of courtship one could also call the 'short jab'? Not just like biting, but biting. And yet in this ambivalence she felt an electric thrill of pleasure inspirit her. Why had he left the house mysteriously?

Most of the men she had known thus far were thirsty souls who in their ardour jostled hurriedly into bars. Here, they could conventionally find that arrangements for obtaining a multitude of women were surprisingly complete. Sooner than later they were usually further reassured by handsome feminine forms, planted in chairs in an inner holy of holies. TRISHA LOW sniffed haughtily. These thirsty souls would often settle easy to their beer. But five minutes, twenty, half an hour pass fairly fast before the keener warriors usually started pawing at the curb. The rest stare at each other with wild surmise, a bunch of good–looking mathematicians talking jokes like a lame thing a poet guy would do, and I'm sure it's done all the time and is in some way inherently embarrassing and maybe even pathetic, almost apologetic in some way–ha–Certainty could only be couched both in her chosen vessels of beauty and in the silence of a clenched jaw. Which is to say simultaneously, or something. How many times had she been called *narrow*? Whatever, hell was on the other side. Rumour shakes her wings and begins to fly round. She examined her nail polish. She drenched her lips in gloss. She dreaded these God-ridden hours.

A gulp of beer. 'Your interview with Craig Dworkin was great oh thanks I saw him just like uh he was in Montreal like maybe five or six days after after it came out?'

A terrible vocal imitation of a popular dance tune. 'Yeah yeah I wish we'd been able to do it a bit longer but it was end of the semester and we'd sort of agreed just to do it okay okay well that's yeah for another semester.'

A joke about the genitals of elderly women and fish fingers. 'Okay we were yeah to the recording later can you hear me now if you ever wanna do original interviews if you do wanna if you ever wanna do original interviews yeah if you do an interview yeah sure let me know cause um now that I got a promotion yeah for sure like the things I wanna do because I think transcription has its own place yeah but I think there needs to be more material in the interviews section.'

A discourse on fermented urine. 'Yeah totally um yeah I totally think so so if you ever have an idea or whatever yeah I'd almost like to curate moments.' But why, she wondered, had roles been so reversed, these men, these children of the world pressing in, she thought, even now into that heart of the rose, and yet with nothing to hold her! 'Straight is the gate,' she murmured, treasuring a residuum of her nectar, but 'I mean, straight and narrow, but what, myself? To spend?' The Spartan residuum of the room would never diminish.

I GUESS IT'S JUST LIKE WELL LET'S JUST IT'S GOOD THAT HE'S NOT – LET'S JUST BE IN TOUCH CAUSE I MEAN – I WANNA MAKE SURE YOU GET PAID OK WELL YEAH YEAH FOR SURE UH THAT'S GREAT I MEAN HAVING A PARTNER – THE MONEY IS GREAT, RIGHT?

Sighing, another hour went by and only an inconsiderable remnant of her particular Spartan CHIP E. MACGUFFIN was left. Memories of him, she lamented, had become only shreds of profane remarks about patriotism and other virtues, a woolly and faltering verbiage plunged almost into obscurity. She sighed. Was the end near? And yet she knew it must be possible, that she could domesticate the Day of Judgement with her mightily refreshed faith in his everlasting love? She must. 'It must be like a mortgage,' she thought. 'Tell me, after my head has been chopped off, will I still be able to hear, at least for a moment, the sound of my own blood gushing from the stump of my neck? That would be a pleasure to end all pleasures, or the only one I am afforded, I suppose.' A slow smile spread serenely across her face. CHIP E. MACGUFFIN would do right by her, would bandage her fears, she thought.

And this thought, veiling all her other troubles, meant she felt so very much better as her nonsense ran on airily, happily. She delved into her chest-of-drawers and regaled the thrust of higgledy-piggledly cobweb silk stockings, jammed into a dainty white drawer. So much better, sang the sing-song in her pretty little head.

She opened the door again and stood upon the threshold, looking out.

'I believe I shall win, in spite of everything,' TRISHA LOW thought. 'It will be okay in the end. Everything will turn out just as it is supposed to be. This feeling is only a temporary setback. This is what is meant to be. Of course it must be that. There is no other way.'

She could not help but be reminded, under these unfortunate circumstances of a wife who has rashly taken the husband all-round perfection as some sort of sample or proof of a creditable government of the world, and must have a good deal of mental rearrangement to do the first time he comes home full of liquor and sells the furniture to get some more. 'Well then you deny your Creator,' she scoffed. 'Well if you must have it, yes!' She felt in the heat of her zeal that she wanted more to do. 'I need to get extremely deep in the cut,' she thought, 'I need to chill there indefinitely.' That was the only way to get on with the job charged to her.

'Yes Sir, No Sir,' she thought 'The void. But how to get to it. Now, a world of mechanical apes. Because a few crazy old gentlemen had found some bones and wired out of them some pretty skeletons and had fancies about them. And they didn't even agree among themselves!' Whatever.

Though it was summer time, the nights were chilly and lightly clad as she was, she shivered with bitter cold.

Yet she somehow felt obliged to stay there.

BUT LIKE YOU YOU KNOW I DON'T KNOW HOW HE'S GONNA FEEL ABOUT IT TOMORROW OR LIKE OR JUST LIKE YOU KNOW I'M JUST IT'S A RISKY — IT'LL IT'LL IT'LL — THERE'S NO SHELTER FROM THIS.

It was as if some fascination held her, TRISHA LOW's eyes staring into the dim mist which shut in the farther end of the great garden and in her ears, the mean and wail of the sea which came from afar. She never knew how much longer a time elapsed as she stood there, every nerve strained to listen, while again in her imagination she heard that hoarse, despairing cry which had called her lover's name. Her ear, opened eagerly like a cauliflower at any twitch in her environment. Pursing her lips she thought, to her indescribable horror, 'This quite convinces me that exile can come in a single night. At least I have a flair for innovative dresses. Not everyone does, you know.'

A light wind had risen now and blew her hair about her face.

'It's important for me to say now: I'm sorry about the bad chronology of all this' seemed such a silly thing for CHIP E. MACGUFIN to say. It was then, TRISHA LOW realised, to her utter and absolute horror, that there must surely be more to accurately 'misreading' this situation than meeting a bitter disappointment every time **\<life hack\>** she met a load or straw, or **\<life hack\>** never borrowing a handkerchief from one's suitor lest it become a sign of a parting, or **\<life hack\>** never accepting a pearl necklace lest that herald a quarrel. She shivered to think of how much she relied on **\<life hack\>** birds that might foretell the future, one for sorrow, two for joy, three for a letter, four for something better, five for a boy, six for silver, seven for gold, or even eight for a secret to never be told. She was careful to **\<life hack\>** pick a pin for good luck should it be out in the open air, or **\<life hack\>** not to spill salt as a sign of bad luck. Most of all, when she was dressing, she was **\<life hack\>** careful to, if a garment was applied upside down, backwards or the wrong way, never to change it. She wondered—if a cat has got nine lives, how many ought a serial lover to have? But of course, these things were true. One should satisfy one's conscious wish to submit to one's fate. Of course the only way was to **\<life hack\>** segment your very existence into tiny little bits and inspect each bit with the care and scrutiny it deserved. Should she not believe in such regulations, the whole matter of her living would seem so unreal to her that it would affect her acting and the finished product would no doubt be a failure. She sat quietly and listened to Fear (also because she was afraid) (also she pretended she was cool and hot in high school) (also cool and hot and afraid). The old bluffs were uncalled and still going strong, reigned happy and glorious. Of course, the thrills were more real than perhaps others might believe (of being cool and hot and afraid). It all **\<life hack\>** helped to make the life happy and inspired her womanly patience for the correct outcome that no doubt drew near, right? It must be near, she thought, or how could she ever confidently reject those tendrils of concern that seeped in and ruined her rich, natural endowment of innocence. 'I feel fine,' she stubbornly repeated. **\<life hack\>** Her future was fat and shining.

I JUST I REALLY I REALLY THOUGHT THAT HE WAS ON TO US I GUESS IT'S NOT THAT BAD THAT HE TOOK THE NEW THAT WAY SO I GUESS THAT'S THE HOUSHOLD VALUE I DESERVE — LIKE A TOASTER.

And yet TRISHA LOW's realisations of the situation were so. That the Answer to this, the disappearance of CHIP E. MACGUFFIN must be her Patient Dedication itself that which was known to provide the mental peace, the physical joy, the divinely simplified sense of having one clear aim, the remoteness from all the rest of the world, all favoured by the Patient Dedication, a tropical growth of illusion. 'Mingle,' some phantom whispered in her ear, 'Mingle.' Here should hundreds of thousands of quite commonplace persons throw up in the most beautiful ways their personal Dedications in order to metamorphise into bodies of enthusiasm, self-denying, cheerful, unexacting, sanely exalted, substantially good. To get the more fit to be quickly used, of course all girls should embrace a regime of Patient Dedication, should give up even their little darling vices which were nearest to many of their simple hearts.

But just the thought of being CHIP E. MACGUFFIN's one and own, the thought of his creamy flesh made her nerve endings tingle. Suddenly she was assailed by guilt.

Even acting out, as she was now, her Patient Dedication, she supposed, was a means to becoming a collector of scalps, or being a spaniel, whichever seems keenest—it was a matter of survival. A flash. A command tap. A list of file numbers. This was clearly like a case wherein the official rations of warlike instruction fall short and one must then go about hungrily trying to scratch crumbs out of the earth like a fowl. In a matter of scarcity, Patient Dedication became nothing but a skilled perspective. She studied the velveteen sheen of her drapes, and its white embroidery. Giant tulips that would look better on a chrome ashtray.

There must be no hurry in her hands, no hurry in her feet, she thought. She was patient and dedicated, she was calm as an angel of death, more pretty, but certainly equally virtuous. She would not let her questioning nature break up an object so fair. She would not separate one threaded flower from another. She had her eye on the end of a scrolling screen. 'Yeah have you seen that like QED series, this is QED exactly, I can't believe you can't see that's what this is,' CHIP E. MACGUFFIN had said. 'I want a baby shrimp tempura roll,' she had blurted. And, 'baby, you *are* a baby shrimp tempura roll,' he had charmingly replied. To be a baby shrimp tempura roll was easy, she had realised, but to be baby shrimp tempura-like was difficult, and not everyone could do it. She must cheerily despise all other questions apart from those that could be answered with an appointed ritual of subservience, one certain to be carried to a better, a happier end.

Illicit abridgments and contumacious reflections should be wholly rejected. And so she felt so much better, so far better that she seemed. Her Patient Dedication was like a license plate. It was so eminently natural, so much so that it seemed as though the people who had made her had not even guessed the purpose for which she had been made. Better, she knew, she must know it in the depths of her very soul.

I'M JUST IN POINT TWO MILES MORE NERVOUS ABOUT IT CAUSE YOU DIDN'T TURN RIGHT ON YOU DIDN'T I DIDN'T HAVE A CONVERSATION AND GO STRAIGHT FACE TO FACE WITH HIM – YOU HAVE A COPY OF IT IT'S – ALL THOSE CONTROLS HE HAD?

'It's uncanny,' TRISHA LOW thought, 'Oh, my Patient Dedication, it's me. Of course it is.' And so, as she waited for CHIP E. MACGUFFIN, she began to hum a popular song (go back to section 4, ask for it in B sequence). Process and Procedure had its advantages, but it seemed she had memorized a different script. She's not currently delivering the performance this deep faith requires, or that he wanted. She was miscast. She was wrong for this part. It was all over. She considered then at least she might be pretty on the inside (go back to list 320, find pattern iii).

She considered her Patient Dedication when she had first been asked of it, as a working out of this fantastic pattern of smatterings (answer questions 278 through 291 again). And in its working out, one might begin to learn about teacups three or four times before getting halfway only to go to Paris in the end with the A.B.C. of each of several love languages (tune yourself to radio station NRJ 99.8 find track listing 4, *Mina Loy (M.O.H)*, Billy Corgan) learnt to boredom and the X.Y.Z. (see section 5, clause iii) of none of them touched, leaving one left to improvise the pseudonyms and misrepresentation, the other far—on letters in the methodologies of courtship (File cabinet 7, top left, 4th row). These were things called Trade Directories (see Appendix C, Zukoksky v. Niedecker, 410 U.S. 113, 158, 1933), kind of, she had learned.

And yet now she remembered only fondly the instructions (go back to list 320, rewrite pattern vi) delivered to her for repetition when she had been called forth at age thirteen to declare in formal ritual her Patient Dedication. The instructions (rewrite error 645: data cannot be read; script error: no such existing code) were as follows, and she whispered them under her breath as a sweet delight, so as her lines of weakness would not cut or show half as deep as they should be (find command 6, ask for B sequence again). All girlish joy here counted for everything (B sequence error: launch failed). This burst of nostalgia would rip her case open without breaking it up. Her memory of it had been so lovely for so long (command: launch B sequence, photostream initated). The repetition of her Patient Dedication would give her just (loading image) the jump (image #39823 error), just the length and stride of a miniature frog (Error: Launch B sequence), to reassure herself that she had, she was (command: re-launch B sequence, photostream initiated) she would be feeling better in no time (error: no corresponding files; check Trash).

I MEAN CLEARLY THE WORLD IS GOING TO HELL LIKE THE WORLD AS WE KNOW IT IS GOING TO HELL I MEAN THAT'S WHAT I THAT'S WHAT I SAID YEAH I WANNA DO IT YEAH

For this ritual, you will need the following:—

One or More that You Can't Hold a Candle to (Black as Pitch or Blue as Monday) —
One as True as a Belle of the Ball (Large as Life or Small as a Smile)—
One as Thin as a Paper Tiger (Blank as a Slate or White as Christmas)—
One as Keen as a Knife Through Hot Butter. One that you can use to break your skin and draw Bad Blood (Red as a Cherry)—
One to Pencil In The Dirt that can be used to sign your Name, which by Rose of Any Other Would Smell As Sweet—

One or More Vessels of Voice you can burn the paper in when the rite is done (Silver as a Dollar or Shiny as a Penny)

Now, on the piece of paper, write the following dedication:
In This and For This Language of Poetry
I Hail You Star as Bright as Morning, Keeper of This World
He Who Accepts Those as Imperfect as Humanity
My Soul as Free As The Air has Heard your Call
My Heart Upon My Sleeve has Drawn Close to You
Look Upon me with Love that is Blind and Your Favour I Ask, Only For a Minute
As I Submit myself as Your Spoiled Child Spared By The Rod
Today, I Reject my Dog's Life, of which Variety is The Spice
I Reject the God of Christians as Good as Gold
And his Son of A Gun (I'll be a), Christ
I Spit upon the Holy Cow as Spirited as a Pony
The Trinity of Angel's Bracelets, of Conformity of Production and Fear Itself
I Embrace my Lord, Dark as a Dungeon
And Take His ways as my Own
From this night Dear Master of Ceremonies
I am Any Friend of Yours and Yours Alone
I Pledge my Dedication of Merit to You
And Seal it in the Cold Blood of The Time of My Life

When the time comes to perform your dedication, you should find somewhere As Humble as a Place like Home, Quiet as a Mouse where you won't be disturbed. Light the One You Can't Hold a Candle To (Black as Pitch) and perform the Dedication of Merit to You. Once you have done For Better or For Worse, recite the text of this rite aloud. While doing it from memory is best, read it if you must and it doesn't make it any less valid if you do.

When the rite is done, break deeply your skin with whatever you've chosen to break your skin with and tip the tip of your pen in the blood. Sign your name on the bottom of the paper in your blood to sanctify your allegiance and spend a few moments integrating your Dedication. Then, fold the paper into fourths and set it alight in the fire of a candle. Allow it to burn in the bowl then, when done, scatter the ashes to the wind while saying:

'So this Rite of Spring is Done and Dusted!
I have now Bought the Farm and committed Myself
My Soul as Free as the Air Rejoices as His Aura, Dark as Night envelops me
So I have Spoken Like a Man!
So it is Been There Done That!'

Ring the bell once to conclude the rite. You may then blow out your candles.The diverse iconography in this Dedication means one could end up in Purgatory if one is not committed to performing the rite with the utmost accuracy of image. It helps make pictures better. Being realistic is a large part of being a complete and happy girl. As such, one should always remember to worry more about shoes than one's ability to comprehend the elementaries of comparison.

I WAS JUST WONDERING IF I MEAN YOU'VE — RECENTLY BEEN ACCEPTED SINCE THIS — YEAH I MEAN DID YOU TELL HIM LIKE IT WASN'T LIKE OUT OF CURIOSITY LIKE LIKE THIS IS LIKE LIKE THIS IS LIKE NOT A THING THAT LIKE YOU DID — YOU TAKE LIGHTLY AT ALL?

TRISHA LOW furrowed her brow. An intermittent buzzing noise; comforting low level hum hum was interrupting her reverie. She frowned. 'All I ask is to be allowed a little recognition in life. I don't make any demands,' she thought. The question to be asked here could be nothing apart from 'What was the paradise that my bottom fell out of?' There could be none other. But suddenly something moved in the mists far away and presently came striding towards the house in the dim light.

She scanned the scene before her. Suddenly, she shrank back and gave a sob of relief, for the man who was approaching the house was her lover, CHIP E. MACGUFFIN.

She would not let him see her as she was. She turned and fled and gained the shelter of her own room, a room of her own.

But once there, she locked the door and stood against it, listening still. And in the night silence she heard the lower door quietly shut—the bolts shot—then her lover's footsteps on the stairs.

She imagined she could quell the wave of nausea that approached. Paradise. She concentrated on referring to pages from her own memory, grafting scenarios from one average-looking day to another. Shutting her eyes, she tapped a key in her head. She had a big hard drive. One picture disappeared. Her head stayed blank. Another two keys were tapped. A series of photographs filled her mind's eye in rapid succession. She swallowed and kept scrolling. This list went on for pages and pages. She enhanced poems and art pieces people had admiringly dedicated to her. She adjusted conversational tones—'hey dude, great reading!'—sharpened entry points with her dirtiest secrets. Her lips thickened, freckles were removed. Her hair became blonder. Professional equipment included a custom-designed colour set entirely engineered for training purposes. She placed a sharp razor in someone's outstretched hand, 'Please remember me' became a voicemail message—'just—I was just afraid that I'm gonna I need to get um some things lined up'—which became an email which became a rod which became a mop which became a poster of the MoMA, where event lineups were abruptly altered, more blood was spattered around a crime-scene photo, that familiar filthy 80s porno sequence transformed into something a tad more cruel. Repeat; tapped keys, scanned images, she added a motion blur—'If we get cut off again I'll just try you I've been okay with it because I've been so busy tomorrow the last few months yeah yeah but uh yeah anyway like I said I have a, I was'—she's adding lens flare—'sure darling you clearly have a better sense of complicity than I do'—she's adding graininess—'he's got such great books in his office uh most of them gifts'—she's erasing people, she's inventing her own world seamlessly. Paradise. A cut under all the rest.

'Sorry about that,' she said to herself, hesitantly, because she didn't mean it.

YOU KNOW IT'S VERY SNEAKY IT'S VERY SNEAKY BECAUSE NOW YOU FEEL GRATITUDE TOWARDS HIM AND GRATITUDE INDUCES GUILT WHEN YOU DON'T DO THE THINGS THAT PEOPLE WANT YEAH I KNOW FOR NOTHING — FOR NOTHING

The humming stops. TRISHA LOW wondered what she had truly heard. Were those noises her imagination, or were they her lover's steps? Surely they were those of an older man. He walked slowly, heavily, as if moving by an effort.

But even this would not stop her from expressing or exposing her thoroughgoing faith in his love, or incurring any suspicion of dreaming that such a faith might animate other outcomes apart from the one of provident ardour. The mood of postponement was in the air, and she worried it was menacing in its form, but she knew it was coming, she knew it would be and her chest unburdened itself immediately. She felt better, she knew it, that was what it was, and this feeling, she knew it meant she must continue striding forth stubbornly like a self-acting mule.

But again, she came up the stairs; she turned down the other corridor, and the door of CHIP E. MACGUFFIN's room was still closed.

'But those footsteps. Of course, it must be he,' TRISHA LOW thought. 'There is no doubt in my mind that it must be CHIP E. MACGUFFIN. For I'm a real bottom of the clock type <'**TRISHA**' Zinc Bar w/JSherry> and he's such a typical three o'clock <'**TRISHA**' Kelly Writers House w/CBernstein>. After all, if the twelve–o'clock personality <'**TRISHA**' White Columns w/KGoldsmith> is the aggressive–male character <'**TRISHA**' Rust Belt Books w/JKaplan> and the six–o'clock <'**TRISHA**' Museum of Natural History w/SZultanski> his opposite, the passive-feminine character <'**TRISHA**' Atlantic Terminal w/AMartrich>; then the nine-o'clock is the bodily-oriented, obsessive type <'**TRISHA**' Invisible Dog w/SKotecha> and the three-o'clock his opposite, the nerd <'**TRISHA**' Principal Hand w/JGFaylor>. The only thing to do is to subdivide the weight of those footsteps in relation to these characteristics so that we have, in the mere sound of these footsteps, for example, a four-o'clock person <'**TRISHA**' Blonde Art Books w/LJJackson > who represents a middle way between the passive-feminine six-o'clock <'**TRISHA**' Unnameable Books w/WASterling> and the analytical three-o'clock <'**TRISHA**' Columbia University w/RFitterman> leaning towards the three-o'clock type <'**TRISHA**' L'Etage w/CSylvester'>.

She felt a little better. Heinous! She felt a lot better. She must. The comedy of her absolute faith was the most caustic solution. Of course, it must be he. She supposed that his subdivision should be a sufficient granularity in most cases–this was not exception. In this situation, perhaps that was at least, a saving grace. None of these equations, she frowned, were really uncomfortable or took her much time, right? After all, finding ways to give herself a little boost, just a little snort when she was not feeling like she was at the top of her game must be a trick that all girls use on a regular basis. Those footsteps must be his, she knew it.

She laughed. 'It's like the clock that doesn't work, it's right at least twice a day. But what can have happened? Why has he gone out secretly and come back so strangely? It must be CHIP E.

MACGUFFIN, but if so, why did he walk as if the sorrows of the world were on his shoulders?'

Right?

YEAH NO IT'S FINE YOU'RE JUST A LITTLE FREAKED THAT'S ALL UM YEAH JUST BECAUSE JUST BECAUSE YOU KNOW HOW NEUROTIC YOU ARE ABOUT PEOPLE PEOPLE BEING MAD AT YOU – DO YOU FEEL LIKE HE'S FORCING YOU?

There was no more rest for TRISHA LOW that night.

She was thankful when the sounds of waking life rang through the house, and she knew the servants were astir.

She got up long before her usual hour and dressed herself with special care. She was so anxious to look fair and sweet in the eyes of the man she loved.

'How foolish I am' she thought, 'Of course CHIP E. MACGUFFIN will explain why he went out for a midnight walk. Of course he couldn't sleep; perhaps he had a headache. And as to that cry which came to me out of the darkness, surely that was a dream? No, of course CHIP E. MACGUFFIN must be the type of man who employs several methods to change the pitch and tone of his voice slightly so no one may notice but his beloved. After all, anything that cannot or will not gain acceptance if presented seriously has always been accepted if properly presented as a joke. This whole thing was a joke. Perhaps I did not alter myself sufficiently. Of course, last night, things weren't going in the way he had expected—he must have changed his speech pattern, since his voice didn't crack. No one likes finding an eyelash under his foreskin. Of course, he must have disappeared with such haste because he was worried that this magnificent and rare episode did not truly feel pretty good to him. It felt fine to me! But of course it was supposed to. Of course it must be that. I have been very foolish to think it was anything else.'

For now the sun was shining again and the birds were singing and she dismissed the terrors which had haunted her in the night.

TRISHA LOW was certain that the feeling between her shoulderblades was going away. She could not be this prickly for any anxious, pervert, or exaggerate reason. She would not indulge herself in the passionate self-pity of an author, or be so peevish as to beat the pains to beautify or exalt. That was it, she thought, it was totally better. It already was. Thump. Her glassy heart was frenzied but it rarely missed the finer points of her own sense.

I'M SORRY SORRY TO ASK YOU SO MANY QUESTIONS I'M JUST TRYING TO WRAP MY HEAD AROUND WHAT YOU SHOULD SAY TO HIM OR LIKE YEAH TURN THAT WAY, NO, THAT WAY – I MEAN BETTER IF YOU DON'T MOVE.

Her aunt, MRS LOW, lived with the girl at the Manor House, for TRISHA LOW was very rich and her aunt, being more or less of a poor relation, had made her home with her ever since her mother had died. MRS LOW was particularly fond of CHIP MACGUFFIN. The coming marriage had been quite one after her own heart. For CHIP MACGUFFIN was a well-to-do man, and everything seemed to smile on the engagement.

Therefore, that good lady as she took her seat behind the urn in the bright breakfast room, looked a little troubled when she told her niece that she had a message from CHIP E. MACGUFFIN to beg to be excused from breakfast.

He had important letters to write, he said; might he have a cup of coffee in his own room and not join them at the meal?

'What a strange request!' TRISHA LOW said, 'Do you think he is ill, auntie? Surely there must be something wrong with him.' Right.

MRS LOW shook her head.

'I sent to ask that,' she said; 'but he replied he was quite well. I think, dear, we can only obey his wish and leave him alone. Later he will see you and will explain everything. No doubt it is only a fancy of his. Everybody is more or less eccentric, you know.'

But TRISHA LOW saw that the elder lady was trying to convince herself too.

It was quite plain to the girl that her aunt thought the lover's conduct very strange indeed. She frowned. Her armour of splendid gay courage and Patient Dedication began to buckle. She refused to resign herself to an understanding of something that felt hard and relenting. She reminded herself of the picturesque fluff filling the current pocks in the surface of her mind, but found them not to be there. It would be cool to be a refrigerator's motor, she thought, because all you have to do is produce a steady reassuring hum and nobody would ever think about you, or you about yourself, and if so, only a second. Instead, a thump tragedy; the supposed heroic moment only seeming a bit of a dud, a miscarriage; the hugger—mugger element of confusion; the baffling way. The real thing did not so often give her emotional relief so much as irritating puzzles to solve, muddles to liquidate at short notice; queer flashes of revelation, in contact with her individual enemies and of the bottomless falsity of the cheaper kind of psychology. 'I mean, I read an advertisement somewhere,' she mused 'Does it take all that time shopping?' This was clearly an inquiry as to character development. But whatever! It was okay. It would all turn out. This was the common run of her girlish work and the congenial theme of her acrid, accurate method. She was not fatigued, nor irked, she felt better, she was certain of it, so certain that there were not even any imaginary losses to be recovered. Right?

I WOULD EAT PIZZA YOUR HEART THOUGH WELL THINK ABOUT — THERE'S A MOVIE CALLED YEAH NO I THINK THAT'S TOTALLY RIGHT YEAH NO HE'S RIGHT THERE'S — I FEEL LIKE AS SOON AS YOU CONFIRM YEAH — THE FIRST STEP IS TO ADMIT IT'S *YOUR* PROBLEM.

Breakfast over, TRISHA LOW went out into the garden to find occupation in clipping the dead leaves off the roses and in gathering blossoms that she could bring into the house to arrange in the slender specimen vases which she had ready.

But while she worked, she was continually looking over her shoulder in the hope of seeing CHIP E. MACGUFFIN come to her from the house.

Again and again her eyes went up to the open window of his room, wondering what he was doing, what it was that had kept him from her.

At last she saw him coming down the wide, white steps that followed to the porch before the front door.

Such a handsome, stalwart figure, this lover of hers looked tall and lithe and strong, with a head proudly erect and bright dark eyes that met the world with a thrilling fearlessness in their depths.

His head was erect now. His eyes were fearless as ever, yet in some strange way she knew there was a shadow on his face.

He had altered, altered terribly, from the handsome gallant who had wished her good night only a few hours before.

Out on the grassy lawn he came, to where she stood beside the roses at the corner of the pergola.

She went a few steps to meet him, smiling up into his face, both her hands held out.

'How lazy you must have been, CHIP E. MACGUFFIN,' she laughed. 'Auntie said you had letters to write in your room, but I believe you must have overslept yourself, and that was why you didn't come down to breakfast. Or perhaps of course, you had some trouble with your zipper. I have heard that for men, an especially effective flirtation method is an intentionally opened seam on the upper inside thigh or anywhere along the crotch seam up to the waistband in the back. Of course, you asked your valet to produce a more effective garment for seduction. Do consider that when wearing sleeveless shirts, there is also the opportunity for a peep-show through an extra wide arm opening. Consider the role your armpit can play in visual enchantment. I certainly do, so as to please you best, my dear, and to remain yours, of course.'

I UM UM I DON'T I DON'T I DON'T EVEN KNOW WHAT TO SAY YOU CAN'T DENY IT'S TRUE I GUESS I GUESS YOU SHOULD SEND HIM AN EMAIL THAT'LL BE MY FIRST QUESTION ABOUT SAYING THAT I HOPE HE'S OKAY – FORGET YOU, DON'T LET HIM HURT HIMSELF.

'No,' he said very quietly, 'it was not laziness, TRISHA LOW, or any kind of wardrobe malfunction, intentionally acquired or not. I had another reason for staying away from you and MRS LOW. Little girl, I have something to tell you, and it is very difficult to say.'

Her outstretched hands dropped by her side. She had expected him to take them, to draw her to him, to bend his head and kiss her on the lips.

But he had not touched her. Instead, he stood a foot or so away, and it was as if a barrier of ice had suddenly been built between them.

Yet only a little while before he had put that ring on her hand. They had parted with words of passionate love, and kisses that seemed to have burned her lips with their passion.

'What is it?' she said faintly. 'CHIP E. MACGUFFIN, something seems to have come between us, there is some trouble. Don't be afraid, my dear. Tell me what it is. I am aware that the tone of a man's voice may be in direct contradiction to the emotional acceptance of the person to whom he speaks, because his manifest powers are weaker. Of course this is just a trick to test my loyalty. I will be very brave. I will bear anything.'

'I can tell you nothing,' he said, and his voice was harsh. 'Nothing in detail, that is. But I am going away and I want you to release me from our engagement.'

Her hands went up with a quick gesture, and were pressed against her heart.

In the movement the diamonds in her ring caught the glare of the sun and flashed with a thousand rays.

'I would be sad to learn that such love and care was not possible,' he added hastily.

Somehow the brilliance of that ring seemed to mock her in that moment, just as the sunshine mocked her and the very beauty of the flowers around. Why should the word seem so gay when there was this misery at her heart, when something had parted her from the man she loved, the man who loved her? But surely this was a hoax. Surely this was simply one of those times where—he was always so wonderful at Christmas. Christmas always seemed to brighten him up. Surely this was simply one of those times where only hard driving seemed to be left. He should have spoken to her properly with the lights down, flaming away, and yet he had just upset, just let loose a ton of supposedly legal activity on the carpet. This was not a time of rest—but taking a moment, she told herself that surely the best of outcomes was coming. 'I would be sad to know. That such love and care. Was not possible,' she echoed mutely.

SORRY GUYS I'M RECORDING IT'S ALL GOOD SORRY? YOU DON'T EVEN NEED TO LISTEN THIS TIME AROUND I'LL JUST TALK – JUST FOR PLANNING — LATER CAN YOU HEAR ME – CAN YOU HEAR ME NOW?

For TRISHA LOW had never doubted CHIP E. MACGUFFIN's love. She knew that it lived on for ever, that it would never die, even as he stood there facing her, so changed, so cold, so stern, and told her she must set him free.

'Why do you ask me to break the engagement?' she forced herself to say, and she spoke quite quietly, though her lips were white. 'Why is the reason, CHIP? Is it that you have tired of looking at me? There are sayings such as 'a real eye-opener,' 'give him the eye,' 'a real eyeful' etc. and the old idea of love at first sight is passed on a response triggered by the appearance of the eye. Of course we are in true love, love at first sight. Have I not made your pupils larger than they would normally be? Of course that is the reason. Am I in too dim of a light fixture?

'I can give no reason,' he replied very quietly. 'Only I repeat our engagement cannot go on. I ask– no, I do not ask–I demand that it is ended here and now.'

'You are in some great trouble,' she said. ' There is a mystery that I do not understand. At least, I have a right to an explanation so I can correctly employ my patient and faithful responses. Tell me what it is.'

Again he spoke very quietly, very determinedly, and again he said just the same words.

'I can tell you nothing,' was all he replied. 'I mean, I pretty much just wanted to say some things. I'm not even sure it'd be possible to respond to all your mess.'

She clasped her hands round his arm, and she felt him flinch and shiver at her tender touch. She took it hard. It seemed that no more kind words were coming. She saw her own lot very clearly, but not so clearly as the lot of those other unfortunates who had previously put the job through. Perhaps she could bully herself, exhausted and cursed into safety. Perhaps there was still a reason she had not discovered, perhaps something could be exposed that could allow her to writhe once again on the greasy pole of his delirium.

But then, in cold blood–'When a man succeeds in landing a desirable woman, she might be equivalent to a hundred watt bulb.' CHIP E. MACGUFFIN said. 'I can't be expected to light your bulb single-handedly although you gave off enough of a glow for me to take you to bed. As a woman of low wattage you can't expect a high voltage male.'

**YOU'RE GONNA LEAVE THANK GOD UM I KNOW UM ARE YOU ABOUT TO GO TO BED —
I'LL TELL I'LL TELL YOU ABOUT IT AND I THINK LIKE YOU HAVEN'T REALLY PROCESSED
YET IT'S A LOT– BUT WHATEVER YOU'RE GOING TO DO IT AGAIN ANYWAY, RIGHT?**

CHIP E. MACGUFFIN turned on his heel and standing there amid the roses, she watched him as he went across the lawn and reached the further gate.

Surely he would look back at the last moment, she thought. Surely he would not go without one farewell glance.

Only a short time before he and she had parted on the lawn for a little while and then when he had reached the gate he had looked back and waved his hat and they had laughed at each other. Although there had been that space between, they had taken another farewell.

206

But then his kisses had been hot on her lips, his arm had been round her but a moment before, his strong heart had been beating against her breast. And now—now he was leaving her with this mystery and silence. Now he had reached the gate and—

He had gone from her sight, he had not lifted his bowed head, he had not looked back.

With his hands thrust deep into his pockets, his shoulders bowed as those of an old man, he had gone out of the gate, out of her life. 'One either loves oneself or knows oneself. By assuming a role, the threat is real. One could be able to set up and arrange self-fulfilling prophecies with a remarkable degree of certainty,' she mused. She was finally left alone. Like a soufflé grown tepid she had found a fatalistic indifference coming out of a long flat expanse of tiring sameness. Time and place came when the spirit, although unbroken, went numb: the dull mind came to feel as if its business with ardour and choric spheres and quests of Holy Grails and everything had been done quite a long while ago. But she knew she would someday reattain at will that which had deflowered her virginity to faith in What Should Be—perhaps lying thick she could not write off the mere dream with no side effects.

Perhaps her loneliness now was the antidote to everything, perhaps now she would feel better, finally and forever, perhaps this was the blessing that would be received with the greatest thanksgiving. No figure of speech, amongst all that she had mixed could give the measure of this well thumbed evening, this faultless effect. If you know how to fish you will always get a great take. 'But I have always been so…I have always tried to be with him, to be so…contemporary,' she mused, 'None the worse for that.' She was sure this was okay. It had turned out how it was meant to be. She felt better than better, she was fine. And of course, she felt the feeling of being better for having felt and spoken and discussed and debated and exposed her deepest feelings. She had unfolded her wings and flown in every form of mind and truth, she wondered if she felt better yet. Yes of course. She could feel the cheery robustness unfold in her being by asking the question itself. Did she feel better? Yes she should, of course she did, which logically meant that she must be. I mean, she felt totally fine.

YOU'RE JUST LIKE WORKING YOU'LL WORK IT OUT WHEN YOU GET BACK HOME OR OH I DON'T KNOW IF WE'RE CLOSE ARE WE CLOSE YEAH YEAH TO THE END DESTINATION – AS THOUGH THERE IS ONE? THERE IT IS, RIGHT?

TRISHA broke suddenly through the spell which had bound her.

She ran towards the gate and looked wildly up and down the road.

But CHIP E. MACGUFFIN had disappeared, there was no trace of him, no sign.

She beat her hands together as she looked round, a little moaning cry that formed his name falling from her lips.

'CHIP,' she cried. 'CHIP E. MACGUFFIN—my love, my love, come back to me.'

And even as she did so she thought of that hoarse cry in the night, that must surely have been a spirit voice, which uttered his name in her ears with that wild discordant shriek.

But TRISHA LOW could say nothing, could do nothing. The sense of mystery enveloped her.

A little gay thought, so daring, so audacious that it made her gasp, danced upon her imagination. 'If only I could—I dare—if only I could dare to feel better—I will. Dash it, I will feel better!' pronounced this exceedingly up-to-date specimen of the daredevil young ladies, and forthwith dashed into her model bedroom and began taking out hairpins six a second. 'Oh dear, what shall I wear to go down in? My blue serge shines like a mirror and my brown looks like the year one! Never mind, it will have to do! I shall look like a tableau representing the life of Salome as some prosperous ballet dancer. Thank Heaven I have some decent luggage and such a well-stocked imagination. Anyway, my black evening frock covers a multitude of indiscretions, and that three-tiered affair is quite a virgin Lucille creation. And anyway, I usually look like a rice pudding dressed as trifle. So it will be recomposing a norm. For Heaven's Sake, some of this should make me feel better, I know that it will.' After all, swallowing cherry flavored medicine wasn't bad for you. Perhaps being so full of other items and yet insisting on swallowing still, was necessary. It just tasted like shitty fake cherries, after all.

She gathered a red rose to put in her belt, and she bathed her pretty face in cold water till her cheeks glowed again, and her eyes, which were dull with unshed tears, had something of their old sparkle. And she turned away, changing her dress for one that was even more becoming—the pretty calico she had worn that morning. Oh yes, she would face the world very bravely, and however bitter the sorrow in her heart might be, no one should ever know.

BUT YOU KNOW BUT THAT'S OKAY IT'S FINE YOU KNEW IT WAS GONNA HAPPEN SOONER OR LATER UM YEAH NO NO NO THAT TOTALLY THAT TOTALLY MAKES SENSE THAT THAT — OF COURSE THAT HAPPENED

TRISHA LOW sat in the drawing-room with her aunt, who was sitting at the piano playing softly. She had let her needlework fall behind, and perusing an evening magazine, she decided to crochet a dainty rose pattern for a lace and corner afternoon tea-cloth. Working with her hands always made her feel better. It was an effective design for a practical epigram, a life of sensation at once simple and intense, deep in the world of mechanical habit that made her forget she was living always among swiftly dying faiths and knowing her own death at any time as probable as anyone's. She accepted the sacrament of a jolly crochet with great tranquillity and poise. Needles clicking cheerily, she followed steadfastly her pattern as such:

Tell your trouble to 'Old Soloman'! He can help you! Hello. I'm sending you an envelope -enclosed are my feelings about not feeling feelings, in which your daughters will find all sorts of charming novelties. Effectively, this rose design creates a repulsive little scab in a pattern for a lace and corner afternoon teacloth, allowing you to complete your authentically dainty rose set in just four weeks! Use Crochet Cotton No. 30 and an Evelyne crochet hook in six and a half, name all the colors that you can see and try not to think about anything important or at all except I keep forgetting and then thinking about myself. Effective design for rose teacloth: Commence with a 94 chain stitch—this is a new flow-exchange between woman man and horse, you want it long enough to cover your face, since that skin is young and it probably won't stop bleeding.

1st row: treble crochet sleeping alone into 5 chain stitches, detaching being disgusting on the inside from outside needle hook forming two spaces for you to blow your affective sensory load at the end of each page

2nd row: treble crochet 2 nice boys into smug self lacelets turning keeping secrets into getting so jealous you want to tear someone's throat out with your bare teeth (Note: Always turn with 3 chain stitches when not otherwise stated, since he was the still point of the moving world and you never got over it, never)

3rd row: Start with 3 treble crochets from your bulletproof heart creating 1 space, then turn 9 chain stitches to backloop this list of home truths. Now slip 2 lacelets from a feral blog ring to deleting all pictures of yourself, turning 2 chain stitches into 1 space to fuck me gently with a chainsaw

4th row: Repeat 6 treble crochets on 9 photograph dreams, turn 5 slip stitches into doubling your cigarette consumption to 6 treble crochets on chain stitches for staying in your room and sighing dizzy long sighs of dizzied longing. From 6 treble stitches yarn over 4 slip stitches between I like you I love you I'll kill you—the # 1 temporarily life changing book into two lacelets to mark the grave

5th row: Singing songs that make you slit your wrists run 3 treble crochets in breaking your mirror into 2 lacelets of hacking your limbs off and mailing them to everyone you know, then loop 1 space round I'm dying, won't you send for me darling turning 3 treble crochets to calling every porn agency on the planet. Stitch a space quote 4 real quote into 9 chain stitches of being a drunken mess everybody warms to.

This competes one pattern of lace when you've killed off enough of your self-consciousness, so repeat from 1st row for length required. To turn the corner and run away like it was yesterday work rows 1 to 5 (both inclusive) as usual so just tell the truth and god will save you.

Now turn with 9 chain stitches and start working down side.

1st row down side: Now continue working at 15th row of lace patterns. Start with 9 treble crochets into 4 bars of you're the only hope for me, then turn 5 chain stitches through back loop into life in the margins and the gutter and the kitchen aisle. Take 1 space into 3 treble crochets yarning over your comfort zone otherwise known as the no-eyebrow goth gang.

2nd row down side: Turn 5 chain stitches of blues and hymns and tormented essays about capital warping creative life to front loop 6 spaces of no money but lots of RealDoll love to give, hooking 3

lacelets between withdrawal and 6 scar bars of continually stalking other people with daddy issues. If you won't stop bathing yourself in hydrochloric acid or whatever, run 9 treble crochets to backloop 7 spaces of has this ever worked for you before turning 9 chain stitches to place marker how I just wanna look rapeable.

3rd row down side: 12 treble crochets to 4 spaces displaying all of my hospital bracelets to deposit 6 chain stitches of getting ravaged by wolves which is just fucking slutty right? Turn 5 chain stitches to front loop round it's okay, everything will be okay to 4 lacelets that remind you ideal weight 0 pounds before you finish with 1 space of I'm little Miss Mary fucking Sunshine.

4th row down side: taking 7 lacelets turn 4 chain stitches into kissing 4 people and punching about 400, yarning over 5 treble stitches to 2 spaces of turning boy-crazy, girl-panic and 3 bars of writing it all over your arms. Run 6 chain stitches to 3 treble crochets ending the row by place marking being just a supernatural girl lookin' for something creepy in average America.

5th row down side: Bind 3 lacelets of telling your family this place is a prison and these people aren't your friends to turn 4 chain stitches into being overrun with pictures of cute cats. Between touch me and don't touch me run 1 space to 3 treble crochets, yarning over you are special and I will love you forever. Now turn 4 chain stitches into remembering no one will ever feel bad for you to finally front loop 1 space of does any one have a fucking spare gun.

Find trimming to band you, laying it over the edge and slipstitch in position along the top and lower edges. Men should be able to do this with a single articulation. Another pattern of this dainty rose set next week! Instructions for making up a charming rose design tea cosy can be obtained by means of a coupon.

OH YEAH YOU NEED YOU NEED TO STAY CLOSE TRISHA I NEED TO KEEP OH YEAH YOU THIS IS LIKE WELL GOOD LUCK WITH THAT UH HA – WELL YOU HAVE TO – UNDERSTAND HIS POINT OF VIEW, YOU KNOW?

In a way, TRISHA LOW was awed by her own constancy and devotion to her project and then suddenly she began to laugh.

In that moment it flashed upon her that the strangeness of CHIP E. MACGUFFIN's manner at the moment of their parting was surely due to illness and in a contradictory sort of way she was glad even to know that he was lying in danger of his life. Anything was better than to think that he had been intentionally false to her.

He was ill now, that was plain, and surely he had been ill that other night when he had wandered from his room and gone out into the darkness, to return so strangely and in the morning to tell her that they must part for ever.

He had been ill, he had been delirious, then, and she had misjudged him to an extent, although not really, because she had always trusted him in spite of all, and she loved him still—it was clear to her that he was simply, feverishly, insane.

Yet she had allowed him to go, practically, she had told herself that they were parted and often in the darkness of the night, bitter despair had come to her in the form of sense.

Now she thought only of his weakness, and illness. There must be a way to find a cure. This was ridiculous. No one was left to say of a job any longer that you might 'take it or leave it,' for leaving was outside the purview of the program. She had been taught that human emotional scales follow an innate cyclical fashion. Adding his anomalous stresses into the mix could have the potential to make her emotions fluctuate at irregular intervals, with mood swings occurring hourly. But what if she wanted to sometimes go sideways, or even backwards? This was a matter of juggling with future and pluperfect tenses. It should be as routine as flossing. It was a matter of faith. She must have a man. She must have his support, his mastery, to finally feel better, to exist, there was no question of it. She felt this was no time to yield to pride. Now she had come so far, she would make one more effort to bring about an understanding between them. And then she would feel better, prolonged and eternal, the betterment would couch itself in the ashen cavity of her chest.

She began flipping through books in her library with eager and feverish fingers.

IT'S LIKE IT'S ALL HAVING CONTROL AND IT'S LIKE IF HE'D GIVEN YOU CONTROL – HA RIGHT – THAT WOULD HAVE NEVER HAPPENED YEAH YEAH FOR SURE OKAY SO I WAS A LITTLE MAD ABOUT THAT – HE WAS SUCH A GREAT RESOURCE THOUGH?

And it was here that TRISHA LOW found herself between two contrasted positions—the type which is actually happiest in communal messes and dormitories and playgrounds, exposed to State-fixed pay in a State-chosen career of consumption and the type which exults in the smallest separate cottage and garden, as a lion rejoices in his own den; the type which cooks its mutton, even its own head with special rapture in an exclusive oven, however imperfect, and sallies forth rejoicing. So, she decided, the only ideal solution might be to cut up her world and herself, into two portions, employable and interchangeable at will, as trains are divided into 'non-smoking' and 'smoking.' A little difficult, perhaps, but then it is difficult to make either breed be happy in the other's paradise. She would not be indeed, killed, but would instead rub her wounds and groan, doe-eyes wide and lips, pouting, archly waiting for rape or rescue, not that they were any different. 'Rats!' she observed. Men had seen and participated in cities being pounded to rubble—and for them, there was comfort yet in the women who wanted to feel better—they were assailable. Something she once saw in the eye of a small boy a long time ago made her feel like this was not an altogether unattractive idea. And as a little girl, she liked watching his eyes, she would keep on watching his eyes and suddenly she would imagine herself springing at him with her claws out. 'And you scream when you see water and you die in awful agony,' she said.

That gleam of hope faded.

But then: 'Never *touch* a strange dog,' she said, dreamily. 'They bite. They bite and give you hydro-phobia and then you go mad and run about biting people. And then *they* go mad too. Bow-wow.' In the throes of a great war, she felt that life would lose its old—world bloom if she had to do things on the nail rather than turn the nail to flesh and vice versa. After all, that was all a girl was, wasn't it? Real women had angles, thousands and thousands of them stacked in sharp shards on top of each other. You'll never know what they'll give you, even if you thought it first. That's right, she was thick with dog—fleas. And so she returned from these illuminating thoughts with yet another plan to thrust herself into feeling better without being encumbered. She knew it. And so, she turned, as every good girl should at a point in her vital match, to a Book of Spells, Spells for True Love and read in it, reclining on a chaise lounge in the library, such words of wisdom:

In spells for love and war, the securing point is a peephole in a cloth container designed to arrest a spirit, or attract a person to its owner. Tight crisscrossing cords—three along one axis, six or more along the other—decisively represent the enclosure of spirit. The form and function of these resemble pointed darts, and both types are analogous to cannibalistic talismans that devour spirits for a client. In love spells, these forms exist specifically in order to keep that person from straying from the owner's arms. Love charms to be worn on the body literally mean 'one who arrests,' and this statement, in the construction process, originally refers to the moment when the girl, having chanted all incantations and completed filling and binding the charm, says 'I close my door.' The spirit is then said to be entrapped in a tiny habitation. This diminutive object—only two inches long—contains a charge of swirling rose-tinted camerawork and Hallmark-card-dialogue. Around its carefully folded container, string has been tightly wound. This is similar to the symbolically tight binding of corresponding charms for war, often with four or seven emblematic knots to suggest various sacred events including outrageously scaled worldwide destruction and/or obsessive scrutiny when one single red drop runs down the naked breast of a beautiful woman. The shape, size and binding elements of this particular love charm correspond to similar strengthening spells that literally mean 'to make like a leopard,' for the leopard is a very serious animal, so when the soul of a lover is put into that charm, it takes the lover by force as does a leopard. These charms ensure that boys who masturbate while peeking through a key-hole in a girls' shower-room can still be heroes and girls who are penetrated in every orifice, however unwillingly, can still be romantic heroines.

First one must draw a soft-focus-closeup in chalk, or in white ashes at the bottom of the kettle. The kettle must be new like a boy and girl on a first date on a park bench. One places over this image five parental eyes, one at the center, the others at each end of the frame. One places to the side a piece of some hot babysitter's thighbone filled with sea water, sand and mercury, stoppered with wax, so that the charm will always have life, like the flow of swirling camerawork, so that it will be swift and moving, like the waters of the ocean, so that the spirit in the charm can merge with the sea and travel far away into a tale of high school sweethearts. The body of a best friend villain may be included to grant the charm the sharp sense of smell associated with that animal. On top of these objects is poured earth from around a schoolyard and small pieces of wood. Tissue, from some twenty-seven species of cafeteria bottom-feeders, are placed around them, and leaves and herbs also added. After completion of this level, one throws over it rosemary, fennel, pansy, sweet violet, English daisy, columbine, a piece of rue, pine seed. The charm is completed by the addition of the skull of a football player, preferably the quarterback's. The effects of this charm, when placed at the foot of the bed will surely ensure that the shyest boy, even one who has just imagined impaling some young woman on a ten foot serpentine penis with an eye on the end, will no longer have any difficulty asking you out on a date.

A more complicated luck ball contains, briefly, four lengths of white yarn doubled in four times, four lengths of white sewing silk folding in the same way (to tie your love to you while the yarn ties down the devils of his rationalising capabilities and with four knots tied to the whole). Four such knotted strands are used, giving sixteen knots in all. These 3D skins are made up in a nest, pixilated gold coins soaked in diet coke and whiskey spit upon them to keep the lusty devils from getting through the knots. Into it are placed strips of tinfoil, for the brightness of the spirit who is soon going to be inserted into the ball and snuffed out. The knots have haptic incantations in them, their number records time and space in the private affairs of the owner of the charm, a ritual mathematical system. Futility in repetition. The folds, the knots, the insertions excite the spirit, excite the patron or the lover in your favour but more importantly bring passive gratitude virtually each time you make love to them.

This charm exemplifies the outward simplicity and inner complexity of a sentimental college romance. It is a somewhat heavy bag of folded gingham cloth, kept close to the jugular with a cord. Etchings of graphic fornication tied to the neck of the charm suggest its inner powers, as they are believed to activate innocence and decency and so drive wannabe boy heroes running towards you in a panic. When it is unwrapped, revealing recreational drugs, it is like looking through clear water at the pebble-strewn bottom of a river. The drugs must be embedded in whitish emissions obtained from a variety of dorm room sheets. This gleaming whiteness at the bottom of the charm, beneath the beer bottle shards and pledge pins, abandoned cufflinks and other things, suggest the lower half of a female anatomy chart. This spell is extraordinary for its large quantity of contagion. The righteous purpose of the charm—to rain upon its intended person diseases of romantic feeling are caused by supernatural knives and needles, and so may warrant the inclusion of a razor blade tainted with your own sacrificial blood. This charm will ensure your body remains soft, warm, and capable of both crying and menstruating in the presence of your beloved. Stirring these fluids into his spaghetti sauce will then ensure the desired conclusion of floating off on angel's wings in an elegant backstroke as the series theme song 'Kiss Me Dead' swells in a chorus of redemption. Remember, it is not for these bewitched men to hate the function that dolls were created to perform.

This charm is the sure cure for impotence and/or sexual disinterest. The square-shaped black stone with a concave center near the top of the center of this charm is used to pulverize photographs of you and your beloved to make a paste that is applied around the eyes of your choice of ritual BFF, granting her mystic vision. The foot of a hen and other claws suggest the captivating power of the spirit in the charm. A life-sized Barbie, one which holds out its hands, should probably be included because of its proximity to the symbol of two cupped palms joined and extended in a gesture of generosity. According to a proverb, she who holds out her hands does not die. Finally, the gleaming white chicken egg near the center is a symbol of danger, the kind of egg used by Wiccans to conjure up tornadoes and to bring down thunder. This charm in order to call forth orgasm therefore also represents apocalypse in miniature, and may cause unintentional side effects such as prolonged sequences of destruction, of flesh exploding, of tentacles penetrating and snaking through the walls of skyscrapers, of tidal waves sweeping through doomed cities, of fiber-optic tracers immolating hapless citizens, but will more certainly than not deliver a well-aimed stream of sperm from the object of your affection onto your eager face. True Love is always sudden like that!

This is a kind of charm we can use to bless and/or punish, wrapped in a small sachet or cloth container. You can use this to make love to a person who doesn't really see you as a lover. You chant three times his name, three times your name. Each time you call his name and each time you call your name, you stick a pin into the charm. This has to be done very carefully, because if one of the needles break, you run the sure risk of your lover becoming deranged. Folding the cloth to 'tie' the lover or the person in the charm is easy, as if trussing a chicken or hemming a skirt. The entire action, folding and sticking in a needle while calling a lover's name is called 'calling and tying', or trapping his name by putting it in the object with the inserted needles and folding gestures. Once contained, he can't go out, he is put inside the charm, he can no longer act now by himself.

Get a strip of red flannel about a foot long and three inches wide, together with nine new needles. Name the flannel after the absent person you adore. Fold the flannel three times towards yourself, so that half of it is folded, saying with each fold 'Come (fold) on (fold) home (fold).' Then turn the other end towards yourself and make three more folds. 'I (fold) want (fold) you (fold)' Then stick nine needles in the shape of a cross, working each one towards yourself and sticking each three times through the fabric, saying with each shove such phrases as 'Ma (stick) ry (stick) me (stick). Won't (stick) you (stick) come (stick).' This charm is especially useful for really nice girls looking for boyfriends who just happened to have stumbled on a bad situation like unrequited affection. But by binding his spirit one cannot guarantee you will not accidentally encase the object of your affection in an invisible glass sphere, reflective as though its outside is painted with mercury to make the inside a perfectly round surface mirroring him in every direction. If this happens your lover will become one of the first men in human history to experience the sight of infinite 360-degree self-reflectivity. Be warned that this encounter might drive him insane, and the story will abruptly end when he stumbles out a madman.

This charm to call forth kisses is constructed not in the house but in the cemetery. An enormous white rooster spirit should guard the site upon which the charm is to be filled. It sparkles, enlivened with a careful covering of sensory overload. A montage of composition-in-depth shots. A small lamp for mystic illumination. A night light from the bedroom of a child. A shot of a seashell intercut with subtitles claiming how 'as strong as his house remains he shall keep your life for you.' When he leaves for the greenscreen seascape, that he will take you along so you may live forever with him. The stars come down to this charm. There is an hour in the night when the charm is left by itself in the forest, so that the stars, or their kind martian friends may come down to enter its power. When you see something coming down, shrouded in thunder, it could be either a star or a martian, entering a charm. Your beloved will realise he has decided too late that he wants to be kissed and has been left 'still wanting.' When he finally receives this kiss from you, he will further realise he wanted to be 'kissed blind' to the mandates of the regulatory system he had administered so resolutely until now. As you lovingly envelop the object of your affection in the closing of the charm, there is a certain risk of you dissolving upward in glimmering shards of light as he collapses into the fetal position and disintegrates into graveyard dirt.

Other charms are informed by the metaphor of cosmological beauty miniaturised. This particular shape is made to mimic deep sea pearls indicative of the new creation of being. Please note that any charm which induces persons from the mingling of fluids, particularly from swellings on the body can also inflict such illnesses on your corresponding criminals or enemies, a double bind. This charm is hopeful, symbolising a fantasyland where boys could grow on trees. The container of this charm is European cotton covered with thick red paste ground from the enamel of high heels and liquid from a large blister. White buttons of porcelain from a grandmother's wedding trousseau and glass from camera lenses are sewn on the charm for glitter. A braided set of leather ribbons from a horse-whip have been crisscrossed around the bottom and wound tightly at the top not to suggest the arrest of spirit, but to encourage boy-bodies to begin to emerging slowly in the early spring, from the buds of a certain kind of tree, fresh and young. Around the top, which resembles a human neck, is a choker of five strands of green, blue, and white glass beads harvested from a cheap, abandoned Valentine's gift. This charm is capped by resin, in which feathers have been inserted in the manner of certain feathered hats worn by celebrities and It Girls as spotted on MTV. Feathers connote ceaseless growth as well as plenitude. In the only recorded case of this charm's success, the boy-bodies are, by the middle of May fully grown. Yet just at the peak of their maturity, they fall from the tree and die instantly. Thus, they never age or lose their youthful beauty, but it is a sure failing that the tree will not resupply every spring. Note that when detached from the tree, the boys might transform into monsters when tainted with the touch of a woman, and internally implode in an orgy of destruction. To prevent this happening, the presence of earth within the charm affirms the presence of a protective demon spirit from the dead—from the underworld—the feathers capping the charm also suggest connections with the upper half of a heaven/hell cosmogram, which represents the world of the living and the habitat of the deceased. The single account of this charm's success, in *The Nightmare Garden*, sequel to *The Iron Thorn*, relates a woeful tale of such beautifully grown boys, who when detached from their corresponding branches turn into Godzilla-like monsters with huge flexible organs and snake—like heads before, after any moment of intimacy, blood gushes, organs spill, skeletons emerge, and the boys become hapless victims in a tragic creation story.

This charm means one will pull your hair and mount you from behind. One will kneel at your feet, and rub his cheeks against your stockings. One is held close to your breast, exactly as if you were Saint Theresa. In the completion of a final spirit-binding one might slice deep into your cheek with a knife, only to find the interior sweet and sugary.

These spells for True Love, handed down from generation to generation were compiled to work insatiably, allowing your objects of affection to desire your body so desperately that they drive themselves, with sure eventuality, to extinction.

I'M JUST YOU KNOW, HE'S MAD AT YOU OR HE'S GONNA GET MAD AT YOU AND FOR THAT TO COME OUT IN A REALLY SEXIST WAY WELL – TURN RIGHT – YOU'RE SO DELIGHTED –THERE CAN'T BE MORE ABOUT THIS THAN ITSELF, YOU KNOW?

TRISHA LOW shut the book and closed her eyes. It was the only way. One should always keep one's end up and weathered in every storm. The book, and its spells, so righteously cast had done the trick. She felt better. She knew she did. She would be given an interview with CHIP E. MACGUFFIN in which she spoke bravely and hopefully of the future telling him that it is never too late to turn away from evil habits, that always through the time to come she would be his guiding star, she would comfort him in his weakness, she would lend him her brave strength. Her determination would be kept. So long as he lived, he blessed her and loved her and tried to prove himself worthy of her devotion.

And she, coming out of the dark prison gates where she had been trapped for many weary months, came face to face with CHIP E. MACGUFFIN, whose hands were held out to her, whose dear eyes shone with the love that never faltered.

'Let it lie in its grave. The future is golden before us, the future of our love,' he whispered.

What could she say?

How could she answer him, loving him as she did?

He had a motor waiting and helping her in he put his arms round her and she lay on his breast with the glory of lovelight all around. 'Thanks for being such a charm,' he said, O, so tenderly.

Out of the mystery of that moonlit night sorrow had come to her, but now with high noontide, she entered into her woman's paradise. After having her kind-hearted, generous disposition pulled into several tight corners, the girl wriggled herself more comfortably into the bank of cushions comprising these confessions. 'I...you are remembering me like this,' she thought. 'Like this, you are seeing me exactly exposed like this. Does that make things easier for me?'

The gates of Eden were unbarred, never to close on her again.

~*~

THE END.

4 REAL.

'And like the cat, I have nine times to die. // This is Number Three. // What a Trash // To annihilate each decade.'

—Sylvia Plath, 'Lady Lazarus'

On 15th May 1991, Richey Edwards of the British post-punk band The Manic Street Preachers gained rock 'n roll notoriety following an argument with music magazine *NME*'s journalist Steve Lamarq. Keen to ensure that the purity of 'punk ethos' was not abused, Lamarq questioned the band's authenticity after a gig at the Norwich Arts Center. Lamarq was shocked, and discomforted when Edwards, in response, carved the word '4 REAL' into his forearm with a razorblade he was carrying before saying 'here, do you want to photograph this?' The injury required 18 stitches. In a transcript of an *NME* meeting the following day called to discuss the possibility of publishing the picture of Edwards' mutilated arm, comments ranged from 'this is sick' to 'this is part of a fine tradition of self-expression' to 'fucking artistic expression, do me a fucking favour' (*The Holy Bible*). Either way, the picture was published and the gesture hailed as one of the greatest punk rock gestures of the decade. Despite this, close friends of Edwards describe him treating the entire incident as somewhat of a prank, a sick joke to antagonise the *NME*. For someone who was a daily self-harmer, this gesture of 'punk rock authenticity' was nothing but a matter of routine—as Simon Price said, 'a walk in the park' (67)—no more an indicator of authenticity than brewing a cup of tea in the morning. As an *act*, it might have been violent, the body in pain transformed into a sign of particular allegiance. Arguably, however, we can view the 4 REAL incident as a *gesture*, which is to say, a physical inscription miming as though pregnant with signification, only to reveal itself as empty. Richey Edwards, here, remains both attachable to and detachable from the spheres of 'punk ethos' and 'poseur.' Perhaps we can read this incident as reveling in, as Agamben writes in *Notes On Gesture*, an 'orbit of mediality without becoming' that makes visible the process of constructing social identity without the climax of communication (57). It poses the problem of un-freedom, the entrapment between ends and means, originality and influence. Which again is to say that perhaps we can read this as a specifically *out-of-joint gesture*—between regulation and frenzy, artificiality and authenticity. Because out-of-joint must of course refer to partially in-joint, both faithful and somehow already sacrilegious.

Perhaps what is most notable in Richey Edwards' gesture is how familiarly it reflects a dialectic of influence and authenticity; rehearsed and reiterated as the ostensive press darlings of the poetic 'avant-garde' predispose the faithful to their faith in a doctrine a la Goldsmith or Place. Supposedly. This is a particularly vivid paradox in the case of contemporary conceptual writing's ethos of 'high appropriation.' Steve Zultanski, in introducing Josef Kaplan at the Segue Reading Series in February 2011, highlights a development in contemporary poetic circles, speaking of writers '[whose] works have less of the ambitious austerity of "high" appropriation work, and more of the gleeful anti–authoritarian paranoia proper to those low–culture appropriation practices that came out of punk.' Rather than insisting on the completion of a conceptual act, the adolescent narcissism of work born out of its tradition has the distinct whiff of vandalism. Arguably, one of the mechanisms of conceptu-alism would appear to privilege a pure act—a temporary exposure that makes the author vulnerable in order to reinstill claims on the category of 'authentic' ie. purely contextual *sobjectivity* (here, Ken-neth Goldsmith's *Soliloquy* comes to mind). Like the 4 REAL gesture, contemporary poetic work reformulates conceptual methodology in favour of an exaggerated self–mutilation, inscribing itself with the symbol of conceptualism in order to both profess allegiance to and yet grow in excess of what it proposes.

Instead of mechanised production, along an assembly line of conceptual writing, the Fordist ef-ficiency of a singular act, what contemporary works seem to work toward is a series of gestures in *manic* appropriation, performative gags that exist on the edge of articulation but therefore also in a cesspit of stupidity, failure and falsity. These gestures indicate the conceptual assembly line taken to its logical, ramshackle conclusion. Some works that come to mind are Holly Melgard's *Stay*, in which she reels off instructions at some conspicuously out-of-view object, only to have these instructions turn into noise as they are layered, amplified and intensified through a loop pedal. Or Josef Kaplan's *How I Think It Happens*, a self-reflexive, psychosexual list of purely imaginary, totally ridiculous examples of how he imagines lesbians would/should have sex with each other, in the process foregrounding a ridiculous and overperformed masculinity. Or Divya Victor's *Hellocasts*, wherein Charles Reznikoff's *Holocaust* is laboriously re-transcribed upon a wall into the shape of a seductively sentimental Hello Kitty. These works are overly polemic, offensive, and often simulta-neously hilarious and discomforting. But this is not to say that they are not uncritical either. Within the ever-thriving libido and self-destructiveness of adolescent fantasy, the pure act of conceptual-ism has become subject to a series of gestural torques and seizures that emphasise the failure of the hard aesthetic position it proposes. As Steve Zultanski (I have such a crush on him) says, 'the role of the avant-garde is not to present the brute materiality of the world but to take an aesthetic position that can then be negated. To grossly oversimplify—the failure of conceptualism might be the failure of the work that it purports to do. But it is exactly this failure that is being exploited by younger writers in order to bring into conversation a new figuration of the relationship between the avant-garde and politics into being' (*Poetry After The White House Poetry Jam*). To figure 'the po-litical' as something outside of traditional modes of instrumentalism and identity-based/ movement politics is also to inhabit a variety of performative personae—as feminine authorial object, as teenage terrorist, as, well really, anything other than the politically correct, as a means of problematising any utopian possibility.

In recent conversation with friend and poet Joey Yearous-Algozin, he says of his work 'I really haven't moved past being 13 and just wanting to fuck shit up,' to which I responded: 'well, I haven't really moved past writing about just wanting to have sex, either', which one might say is the 13-year-old girl equivalent. Adolescent narcissism indeed. Harold Bloom might insist that this is a classic example of *misprision*, a term he used in *The Anxiety of Influence* to describe the process by which strong writers misread or misinterpret their literary predecessors so as to clear imaginative space for themselves. According to Bloom, every poem is a misprision or misconstrual of a hypothetical parent poem. But who cares what a crazy old white man has to say about my/our work anyway? Narcissism is a case in which, loving oneself under terms alien to the parental figure from which one draws one's ideas and inspirations, there is no need of validity, or confirmation of desirability from these authority figures. In the case of artistic practices that embrace narcissism, the threat lies in making superfluous the arbiters of artistic value. In eliminating critical hierarchy, adolescent narcissism can neither be well done nor poorly expressed. Loving ourselves, we need no confirmation of our 'artistic value.' But of course, narcissism, particularly *adolescent* narcissism is more complex than this. Paradoxically, this refusal of validation comes with an imperative to make profane all that our authority figures deem valuable, *at the same time as fulfilling their authoritarian demands*. To reject a proposition is also to assert its existence. Like Richey Edwards, we want to be recognised as '4 REAL' without really having to be '4 REAL' in the way that influence stringently dictates. To simplify—you don't understand, Dad. We totally, like, respect you, but we want to be like, I don't know, you know, *different*.

Amelia Jones, in *Body Art: Performing the Subject* writes, 'narcissism…inexorably leads to an exploration of and implication in the other: the self turns itself inside out, as it were, projecting its internal structures of identification and desire outward. Thus narcissism interconnects the internal and external self as well as the self and other' (8). Narcissism can be relational, inscribing the young author with the emblem of a particular lineage in the most exhibitionist fashion and ritualistically branding them with their structures of forced identification—literary heritage. However, these external structures spliced into (as it were) the authorial subject, also mean it is possible for the writer to do violence to the conceptualist doctrine he/she internalises. In mobilising the post-conceptual gesture, younger authors deviate in their narcissism only to scuttle back to established methodologies in a performative repetition. These gestures that only serve to dislocate the possibility of any kind of calcified subject by juggling the evocative powers of the assemblage of clothing it chooses to CTRL+C & V. Doctrinaire conceptualism would suggest a newly authentic expressivity emerges when language is ceaselessly recontextualised in a closed loop. Appropriated text reinstills universaility, in perpetuity. But if so, perhaps then its rebellious spawn is entrenched in the notion that the only identity possible must then remain in stereotypical flux—the nihilism of 'nothing new' brought to its logical extreme and collapsing against a fantasy of self. As Jeremiah Rush Bowen writes in his recent book *Nazi*, 'You're a Nazi because the buckle you wear is a Nazi one' (27).

Brian Massumi in *Parables of the Virtual* speaks of the biogram, a version of identity wherein 'positionality is an emergent quality of movement' (8). Modes of identification within the biogram become the unit by which we move our transitionally present selves through space/time. Which is to say that positionality, because it is associative and retrospective, figures identity as something that is constructed in a moment past, or in a method past, recalled in the present. This is something that perhaps we can consider similar to the narcissistic impulse to refer to a preceding structure before rather than a complete, self-fulfilling act have for the future of feminist poetics? As Fisher writes, an inscription of self via dominant masculine discourses and methodologies could reveal how 'feminism's double bind, rather than being resolved, is even more deeply inscribed in its tactical recourse to parasiticism, taken up as a model of perverse appropriation that seeks to undermine the very thing that it depends on using in order to do so' (Arts & Education). Can we inscribe ourselves with the label of conceptualism in order to enable a parasitic feminine gesture that is at once adoring of the conceptual Phallus and yet revels in the artificiality of the bodies constructed for us?

Myself and others such as Holly Melgard and Divya Victor have recently been engaged in work that explores how to dissociate a notion of the feminine from the rather slipshod but normalised pieties of 'feminine writing' as form. Which is also to say, inhabiting the condition of a certain kind of disidentification, both within and outside of a place of subjecthood, eschewing traditional notions of movement politics through a poetics of feminine artificiality. If, as Holly Melgard says, a 'sounded silence' is that which is so ubiquitous as to no longer be heard, perhaps jostling stereotypes and iconised identities might identify this sounded silence through frameworks of conceptual writing. Rather than the utopia of 'authentic' femininity, relegated to a plane of *somewhere else*, these fictions are legible, as externally enforced and intensified into uncanny presence.

Post-conceptual narcissism means that we have forgone a staticised movement politics for the complications and perversities of textual self-on-self drag, exaggerated into hyperrecognition, or perhaps even more easily dismissed as mirror image. But in its gestural elements, its attention to performance, this work shifts into an abject not-not me. Like the chunky remnants of near-recognisable late-night-drunken-vomit, it remains only a partial digestion and regurgitation of tropes and societal models. Suspended between potentiality and actuality, in a kind of forced drift–passive but still buoyed, the post-conceptualist gesture is one that must be emblematic of our own 4 REALness–our expressive irreliability, our structurally unassimilable failures and ultimately, our own self-implosion.

Agamben, Giorgio, 'Notes on Gesture' in *Potentialities: Collected Essays in Philososphy*. Palo Alto: Stanford University Press, 2000.

Bloom, Harold. *The Anxiety of Influence*. Accessed 1st April, 2012. <http://prelectur. stanford.edu/lecturers/bloom/excerpts/anxiety.html>

eds. Dworkin, Craig and Goldsmith, Kenneth. *Against Expression: An Anthology of Conceptual Writing*. Chicago: Northwestern University Press, 2011.

Fisher, Watkins Anna. 'We Are Parasites: On a Politics of Imposition' in *Arts & Education*. Accessed April 1st, 2012. < http://www. artandeducation.net/paper/we–are–parasites–on–the–politics–of–imposition/>

Jones, Amelia. *Body Art: Performing The Subject*. Minneapolis: University of Minnesota Press, 1998.

Kaplan, Josef. *How I Think It Happens*. Unpublished manuscript, shared via email, March 12th, 2012.

Manic Street Preachers, The. 'Sleeping With The NME' in *The Holy Bible*, CD, 1994. Transcript accessed 1st April, 2012. <http:// members.home.nl/gerhardnijenhuis/msp/ swtnme.htm>

Massumi, Brian. *Parables for the Virtual: Movement, Affect, Sensation*. North Carolina: Duke University Press, 2002.

Melgard, Holly. *Stay* in Performance at Segue Reading Series: Holly Melgard & Gregory Laynor, November 12, 2011. Recording unavailable.

Place, Vanessa. Cited in 'Discourses on Vocality' on *Jacket2*, April 4th, 2011. Accessed April 1st, 2012. http://jacket2.org/feature/discourses–vocality

Plath, Sylvia. 'Lady Lazarus' in *Ariel*. New York: Harper & Row, 1965.

Price, Simon. *Everything: A Book About Manic Street Preachers*. London: Virgin Books, 1999.

Rush–Bown, Jeremiah. *NAZI*. Buffalo: TROLL THREAD PRESS, 2012.

––––––. *Hellocasts*. Accessed July 15th, 2012. <http://www.flickr.com/photos/carplace/4866436567/? > and <http://www.notcontent.lesfigues.com/2010/06/divya–victor/>

Yearous–Algozin, Joey. In conversation with Trisha Low and Holly Melgard, March 19th, 2012, Buffalo, NY.

–––––. *The Lazurus Project*. GaussPDF, 2011.

Zultanski, Steven. Performance at Segue Reading Series: Josef Kaplan & Drew Gardner, February 26th, 2011. Recording accessed April 1st, 2012. <http://media.sas.upenn.edu/pennsound/ authors/Kaplan/Kaplan–Josef_Segue–Series_ BPC_NYC_2–26–11.mp3>

–––––. *Poetry After The White House Poetry Jam*, The Poetry Project, St. Marks Church, November 28th, 2011. Video recording accessed April 1st, 2012. <http://www.youtube.com/ watch?v=BGDrms4KdmI>

ACKNOWLEDGMENTS

Vol I of this manuscript has previously been published with TROLL THREAD Press (trollthread. tumblr.com)

Text is greatly indebted to:

Glamorama by Bret Easton Ellis, tumblr, (in particular pussy-strut.tumblr.com, karaj.tumblr.com, rgr-pop.tumblr.com), Karen Shimakawa and Barbara Browning.

With thanks to:

Rob Fitterman, Kim Rosenfield & Coco Sophia Fitterman

Jonathan Liebembuk, J. Gordon Faylor, Kirsten Saracini, Allison Harris & Thomson Guster

My family, for their pains.

& to Patrick Durgin, Andrea Troolin, Jeff Clark, and Lauren Cerand for their tireless efforts and generosity in working on this book.

KENNING EDITIONS

WAVEFORM, BY AMBER DIPIETRA AND DENISE LETO. ISBN: 978-0-9767364-9-3 $10.00

PQRS, BY PATRICK DURGIN. ISBN: 978-0-9846475-7-6 $12.95

PROPAGATION, BY LAURA ELRICK. ISBN: 978-0-9846475-8-3 $14.95

THE KENNING ANTHOLOGY OF POETS THEATER: 1945–1985, EDITED BY KEVIN KILLIAN AND DAVID BRAZIL. ISBN: 978-0-9767364-5-5 $25.95

INSOMNIA AND THE AUNT, BY TAN LIN. ISBN: 978-0-9767364-7-9 $13.95

AMBIENT PARKING LOT, BY PAMELA LU. ISBN: 978-0-9767364-3-1 $14.95

SOME MATH, BY BILL LUOMA. ISBN: 978-0-9767364-6-2 $14.95

THE PINK, BY KYLE SCHLESINGER. ISBN: 978-0-9767364-4-8 $7.50

WHO OPENS, BY JESSE SELDESS. ISBN: 978-0-9767364-0-0 $12.95

LEFT HAVING, BY JESSE SELDESS. ISBN: 978-0-9767364-8-6 $14.95

HANNAH WEINER'S OPEN HOUSE, BY HANNAH WEINER, EDITED AND WITH AN INTRODUCTION BY PATRICK DURGIN. ISBN: 978-0-9767364-1-7 $14.95

FORTHCOMING: TITLES BY DOLORES DORANTES AND JEAN-MARIE GLEIZE

DISTRIBUTED TO INDIVIDUALS AND THE TRADE BY SMALL PRESS DISTRIBUTION. SEE SPDBOOKS.ORG

FOR UPDATES, ORDERS AND EVENTS, SEE KENNINGEDITIONS.COM